DAN SMITH
BIG GAME

Based on the original story by Jalmari Helander and Petri Jokiranta

2 PALMER STREET, FROME, SOMERSET BA11 1DS

Text © Dan Smith 2015
Based on the original story by Jalmari Helander and Petri Jokiranta
Based on the original screenplay by Jalmari Helander © 2015
Based on the original motion picture produced by Subzero Film Entertainment
in co-production with Altitude Film Entertainment and Egoli Tossell Film

First published in Great Britain in 2015
Chicken House
2 Palmer Street
Frome, Somerset, BA11 1DS
United Kingdom
www.doublecluck.com

Cover and interior design by Steve Wells
Typeset by Dorchester Typesetting Group Ltd
Printed and bound in Great Britain by CPI Group (UK) Ltd, Croydon, CR0 4YY

The paper used in this Chicken House book is made from wood grown in
sustainable forests.

3 5 7 9 10 8 6 4

British Library Cataloguing in Publication data available.

PB ISBN 978-1-910002-79-7
eISBN 978-1-909489-95-0

*For anyone who ever thought they
weren't good enough*

The forest is a harsh judge. It gives each of us what we deserve. We must know how to listen and fight tooth and nail for our prey. This is what we have done for centuries and will do for centuries more. Nothing is given to us for free.

THE FIRST HUNT

Crouched in the shadow of a silver birch cluster, I lifted my head and sniffed the breeze. The earthy musk of damp moss and soil filled my nostrils, but there was a hint of something else; something warm and wild.

I remained still, listening for the rustle of movement.

There.

Something ahead, hidden in the dappled green of the forest.

Without taking my eyes off the trees, I reached down and snatched a pinch of last autumn's leaves. Brown and dusty, they blew towards me when I sprinkled them in the air, and I knew that whatever was out there would not be able to smell me. I was under the wind.

My grip tightened on the bow in my left hand, and with my right, I reached back to slip an arrow from the quiver. Its point was sharp and clean.

Nocking the arrow to the bowstring, I stepped forward without making a sound. I paused, then took another step, moving slowly. Ahead, the forest floor was littered with dry leaves and twigs. But I was a hunter. The best in our village. I would pass over them like a ghost.

Stepping on to the coppery, mottled carpet of leaves, I kept my foot flat. Time stood still. My heartbeat slowed. My muscles were relaxed and my mind was calm.

And then I saw it. Not far ahead. A shape through the branches.

It was the biggest animal I had ever seen, standing proud and straight, its head turned in my direction. Its antlers were enormous, spanning at least as wide as I could hold out my arms.

Straightening my back and taking a deep breath, I raised the bow and drew the string to my cheek. I closed one eye and aimed, allowing my breath to leave my lungs in a steady stream.

Now.

When I released the string, the arrow hummed across the forest. It cut through the air, covering the short distance in an instant: a deadly missile of wood and feather, fired straight and true.

But the arrow clipped a swaying branch and deflected to the right. It twisted and spun, clattering against the trunk of a silver birch and falling into the leaves like a harmless twig.

'Damn.'

Right away I reached for another arrow, put it to the string, drew and fired.

This time the arrow made it through the branches, but its power was gone by the time it reached the deer. When it struck the animal's hindquarters, it bounced off and was swallowed by the undergrowth.

'No way!'

I moved closer and fired again, this time almost hitting the place where the buck's heart would be, but once again the arrow failed to pierce its skin.

'I'm dead,' I said, lowering the bow. 'I'm never going to pass the Trial.'

Reality came crashing back around me. I wasn't the best hunter in my village. I wasn't even the best hunter my *age*. I was hopeless. My bow was weaker than the other boys' because I wasn't strong enough to draw anything bigger, and my aim was worse.

I sighed as I trudged across to the shape behind the trees and pushed through the branches to stand beside it. From a distance it looked just right, but close up it was nothing more than a pile of sticks and moss with an old coffee-coloured blanket thrown over the top. Dad and I had built it last month for me to practise on, right here in the trees behind our house.

I cursed and put another arrow to my bow, and shot the dummy at point-blank range. The tip of the arrow thumped through the blanket and straight into the fake animal's heart.

I shook my head. Maybe I'd be all right if I could get

close to something. Or maybe I'd get lucky, or—

Footsteps behind me.

I turned and waited, knowing it was Dad because I recognized the timing and weight of his steps. He was a big man, with a long stride, but was light on his feet.

'Oskari,' he said, holding the branches aside and looking through. 'Getting in some last-minute practice?'

I brushed the hair from my eyes and shrugged, trying to ignore the creeping sense of dread at what was to come. Tomorrow was my thirteenth birthday, but before I could become a man, I had to face the Trial.

'Well . . .' He hesitated, as if he didn't quite know what to say. 'Everyone'll be waiting. Are you ready to go?'

'I guess.' But I stayed where I was.

Dad watched me for a moment, then came over and put a hand under my chin, lifting my face so I had to look at him. 'It's okay,' he said. 'You'll be fine.'

I nodded, and tried to smile. But it didn't feel like I was going to be fine.

THE PLACE OF SKULLS

My stomach was turning somersaults as I propped my bow in the corner of my bedroom and left the house.

Dad was waiting in the SUV, with the engine already running. He was drumming his fingers on the steering wheel. 'Come on!' he called through the open window. 'We have to go.'

I pulled the front door of the house shut behind me and jogged over to the vehicle, but when I went around to open the passenger-side door, Dad shook his head at me.

'On the way to the Trial, you sit in the back,' he said. 'When it's over, you can sit in the front like a man. It's the way things are done.'

Without replying, I climbed into the back. It was a long time since I'd sat there, and it made me feel small.

Dad crunched the SUV into gear and drove away. He glanced at me in the rear-view mirror and ran his fingers across his beard as if he was thinking hard about something. 'I know you don't really want to do it, but tradition is tradition.'

'I *do* want to do it,' I said.

He opened his mouth to speak, then thought better of it and closed the window instead. Right away, the cool breeze stopped and it felt very hot in the back. The air was stale and smelled of old boots.

Through the village, the pot-holed road was lined with waiting vehicles, and as we passed them, they beeped their horns and fell into convoy behind us. I tried to forget they were all following *me*. They were coming to *my* Trial.

'Do the elk,' Dad said.

I took a deep breath, cupped my hands around my mouth, and tried to make the sound he had taught me. *'Myygh! Myygh!'*

Dad frowned. 'Well, it's close, but sounds a bit more like an old man snoring. Maybe your deer is better?'

When I tried to make that sound, though, it was more like a drowned cat. Dad shook his head and turned his attention back to the road.

I closed my eyes and wished I were somewhere else. 'Sorry.'

'You'll be fine, Oskari,' he said for about the fifth time. But it sounded more like he was trying to persuade himself that I wasn't going to let him down. 'Everything you need is on the ATV. But if you remember what I showed you, you won't need any of it. In my day, there *were* no ATVs to get around, only our feet, and we managed just fine. Now, tell me what are the two most important things.'

'Umm . . .'

'Come on, Oskari. The two most important things.'

'My knife.'

'Yes.'

'And my fire kit.'

'You have them with you?'

'Right here.' I patted the knife hanging from my belt, then touched the pocket of my jacket where there was a waterproof tub containing my fire kit.

'Good boy. As long as you have those two things, you can survive anywhere and anything. Carry them on you at all times. Never put them in your pack, and don't lose them. Out there, they can be the difference between life and death.'

'It's just one night,' I said, trying to make myself sound brave.

'Doesn't matter. One night in the wilderness is enough. Anything can go wrong; you know that. The knife and the fire kit will keep you safe and warm and well fed for as long as you need. And you will have the bow, of course.'

The bow. Just the thought of it made my stomach go cold.

I sighed and turned to look through the dirty back

window, swaying and jostling with the movement of the vehicle. The village was long gone now, lost in the trees as we climbed through the foothills of the tallest mountain in this part of the wilderness – Mount Akka.

Behind us, the trailer rattled on the bumpy road, with Dad's all-terrain vehicle secured to the top of it. The ATV strained against the chains as if it were alive and desperate to break free. With its chipped green paint, that big old muddy quad bike had been around for as long as I could remember, and Dad was always fixing it or trying to trade for parts because he couldn't afford a new one.

Behind that was the line of vehicles following us: an assorted convoy of old rusted pickups and four-wheel-drive SUVs. Some of them were loaded with equipment and covered with tarps that flapped in the wind; others pulled rickety old caravans. I watched them for a moment, and it made me feel sick just thinking about all the men inside them: men who were coming up the mountain to watch me take the Trial, men who were expecting me to fail because I was neither the strongest nor the best at anything.

Mum always said I was a slow grower. When I came back from school with bruises, she would make me hot chocolate and say it was only a matter of time before I was bigger and stronger than boys like Risto and Broki, but that they would never be as clever as I was. Dad would smile and agree.

'Bigger, stronger and smarter,' he used to say. 'You'll be more than just a hunter one day.'

He didn't smile much now that Mum was gone, though.

To the left of the road, the rocky crags and endless pines swept up into the wilderness that rose around Mount Akka. There, the lush spring forest was thick and dark and full of life. Right now, though, I didn't want to think about what lived in there – bears that could take your head off with one swipe of their paw; vicious, dog-size wolverines with teeth that could crush bone. Mum used to tell me stories about other things, too; like *Ajatar*, the Devil of the Woods, who appeared as a dragon and made you sick if you so much as looked at her. And there was the *näkki* that lived in the swamps and lakes, a shape-shifting monster who was waiting to drag you down to a watery death. All just kids' stuff, of course, but I used to love it when she sat on the edge of my bed and told me about them before kissing my forehead and turning off the light. She knew all the stories.

'You're thinking about Mum.' Dad's voice was quiet. 'I can always tell.'

I didn't say anything.

'I miss her, too.' It was almost a whisper, as if he didn't want to admit it.

On the other side of the road, there was a drop that fell away to nothing. If Dad steered too far in that direction, we would topple over the edge and it would be a long time before we hit the ground.

'I have something for you,' Dad said. He popped open the glove compartment and rummaged inside while watching the road and leaning to one side. There were all kinds of things in there: wrinkled papers, cartridges for his rifle, an old knife with a bone handle, loose pieces of twine and an open packet of cigarettes. What he took out, though, was a crumpled scroll of paper, which he passed back to me, saying, 'Here. For you.'

'What is it?' I asked, reaching forward to take it with trembling fingers.

The paper was yellow, as if it was very old. It was stiff, creased from where it had been squashed into the glove compartment, and it smelled of oil.

Dad grabbed the packet of cigarettes and took one out before throwing the carton back in and snapping the glove compartment shut. When he lit the cigarette and opened the window just a crack, the wind blew the smoke into my face. I moved to get away from it.

'Go ahead,' Dad said. 'Open it.'

I hesitated for a moment, then took a deep breath and unrolled the paper to look at the old drawing.

'A map?' I recognized one or two of the places marked on it. I could see the road we were on right now, and the forest that stretched out to our left. And, high in the foothills, at the base of Mount Akka, was the Place of Skulls, where we were headed. Right down at the bottom of the map was our village.

'There's a red cross,' Dad said.

I traced my finger over the map, feeling the ridges and bumps of the old, stiff paper. 'Yeah. What is it?' I kept my fingertip pointing at the red cross. It looked new, as if someone had drawn it with a marker pen.

'It's our little secret,' Dad said. 'A place where there are bound to be deer.' He took his hands off the wheel and stretched his arms wide. 'I'm talking about handsome bucks with big antlers.'

'A secret hunting ground?' I studied the red cross, already feeling the mystery of that place. I remembered how Mum used to say the buck would be my animal – that it was what the forest would give *me*.

'Exactly. So you get close, you wait until dawn, and you stay under the wind.'

'Okay, Dad.' I tore my eyes from the map and looked up at him. 'I know how to call them.'

I saw his reaction, though. The way he raised his eyebrows and looked away to stare at the road. 'The secret hunting ground is on a large plateau near the top of the mountain,' he said. 'Rest before you get to the peak and climb up at dawn. You'll find a buck and pass the Trial.'

Rest. In the dark. Alone in the forests of Mount Akka for a whole night. I'd thought about almost nothing else for the past two weeks. I'd dreamed about it, waking up with a heavy feeling of dread settled in the pit of my stomach.

I swallowed and tried to make myself feel strong – for me *and* for Dad. This was important for both of us.

'Dad?'

'Hm?'

'I want you to know . . . the Trial . . . I'm going to do my best.'

'I know you will.'

I glanced down at the map once more, then rolled it up and stuffed it into my pocket. When I looked up again, Dad was watching me in the mirror.

'But I don't know if my best will ever be—'

'Your best will be good enough.' Dad nodded and forced a smile, but we both knew: Dad was a hero, a *legend*, and whatever I did, my best would *never* be good enough.

The world darkened when the road twisted away through the trees and Dad took us higher and higher into the foothills. We continued up into that explosion of greens and browns, surrounded by pines and spruce that reached so high I had to press my face to the dirty glass and look up to see the tops. The fresh, sweet smell that came in through Dad's open window reminded me of early mornings in the forest. Every day for the last month he had woken me at first light and taken me out to the forest behind our house to practise making fires and building shelters. He'd made me track animals and use camouflage and shoot arrow after arrow at the fake deer, using his bow instead of mine. I'd never been strong enough to draw his bow all the way back, though, and I knew it worried him as much as it worried me.

Dad crushed his cigarette into the ashtray and closed the window. 'Nearly there,' he said.

My stomach reeled and I made myself nod. 'Yeah.'

I shuffled to one side so I was right behind him, and took out the photo I had stolen from the board in the Hunting Lodge. About the size of a postcard, it was old, like the map, and creased down the middle. I unfolded it and stared at the picture of Dad on his thirteenth birthday. With a large bow in one fist, he was hunched under the weight of the brown bear's head he carried on his back.

I wondered how I could ever be as strong and brave as him.

'You'll show them,' Dad said, as if he knew what I was thinking.

I folded the photo away and stuffed it into my pocket just as he glanced up in the rear-view mirror.

'You've got your mum's brains, Oskari. You're smart. Way smarter than I ever was. There's more to this than being the biggest and strongest; I've told you that.'

I couldn't think of anything that would be more useful than being the biggest and strongest, though. The bravest, maybe. Or a rifle.

'Remember the map,' Dad said. 'Don't lose it.'

As the head of the convoy, we were the first to reach the top of the foothills and emerge into the Place of Skulls at the base of Mount Akka. We rattled and bumped on to a large, flat and stony clearing I had never seen, but had heard about from the older boys. It was almost completely surrounded by thick forest and craggy rocks rising up on all sides, but at the near end was a sheer drop, and I could see thick, rolling clouds smothering the distant peaks of the other mountains. Dad drove us almost to the edge, tyres crunching on the loose stones, then turned the SUV and brought us to a stop, facing into the Place of Skulls, before switching off the engine.

At the opposite side of the clearing, a black cloud erupted from the treetops. It burst up into the grey-bruised sky and broke into what must have been a hundred crows. They circled and scattered in different directions before coming back to settle.

When the men of my village talked about this place, they spoke as if it were sacred ground. As if it were a part of them. And even though some of my friends had described it to me, and Dad had tried to prepare me for it, I had never imagined it would look like this.

THE TRIAL

In the centre of the Place of Skulls was a huge platform built from dead pine and birch trunks. It was like a giant crate, and through the gaps between the dark and weathered wood, I could see the surface of smooth grey boulders inside used for support.

It looked like it had been there since the beginning of time – like a great altar ready for a sacrifice – and I wondered how many boys had been brought up here and made to stand on it, waiting to take the Trial. A ring of old wooden stakes circled the altar. Large poles of pine as thick as my forearm and high enough to reach my shoulder. Others were scattered about the area, driven into the earth at random, each of them topped with a skull. Some were small, just the remains of grouse

15

or pheasants or rabbits, but there were other, more impressive skulls here, too. I could see what was left of a deer, a couple of foxes and even the skull of a large buck, complete with antlers. And there, right ahead of us on the tallest pine pole, was the skull of a bear.

Battered and yellowed by the wind and rain and sun, the bear skull was fixed to the top of the pole with its mouth open as if it was letting out a fearsome growl. As if, even this long after its death, it was still angry at what had happened to it.

The skull was at least three times the size of my own, and the great curved teeth were as long as my fingers. Teeth like that could crush a man's head or rip off his arm. A bear that big could break every bone in a grown man's body as easily as I could snap a birch twig.

I shivered and stared at the skull.

The skull stared back at me, hollow-eyed.

'Is that yours?' I asked, shifting in the seat and breaking the silence.

'It is.' Dad nodded and put a hand to the bear's tooth that hung from a leather cord around his neck. 'But it doesn't have to be a bear. Hamara brought a deer, not even a buck. And Davi managed only a pair of grouse.'

I looked back into the dark, empty eyes of the bear skull and wondered what the forest would give me. What did I deserve?

Other vehicles began filing out of the trees behind us, lurching and jostling to where we were parked. They formed a semicircle facing into the Place of Skulls, then the men climbed down from their cabs. Within a few minutes, there were at least twenty of them setting to work as if they each had a job to do.

'Wait here.' Dad popped the door and stepped down into the clearing. For a second, the sounds of the men filled the car, then Dad slammed the door shut and everything was muffled once again. It made me feel different from everyone else. As if I was not one of them.

Dad pulled his cap tight on his head and fastened his green jacket over the top of his hoodie, then trudged across to the last vehicle in the line. It was an old SUV, rusted and falling apart, with a small caravan attached. Hamara, the owner, was standing beside it, with his thumbs tucked into his belt, watching as the other men set to work.

Hamara was the biggest man I had ever seen. He was a good head taller than Dad, with a shaggy grey beard covering most of his wrinkled face, and long, straggly grey hair hanging out from underneath his battered black woollen hat. His camouflage jacket was open to reveal a dirty beige sweater that strained to contain the bulge of his stomach. On his feet he wore a pair of large rubber boots. He carried a rifle over his shoulder that looked as old and weathered as he did.

Dad didn't much like Hamara, always said he was a grumpy old man, but he was the chief elder of our village and there was nothing anyone could do about that.

They spoke for a moment, then both turned to look in my direction. I could tell Dad was nervous because he was picking at the skin around his left thumbnail. He always did that when something was bothering him. The first time I saw him do it was at the hospital, when Mum was ill, and he had picked it raw. He hadn't even seemed to notice the blood.

Hamara watched me with his piercing, watery eyes, and tightened his mouth before nodding once. Dad stood for a moment, then looked down at his boots and came back to the SUV.

'Come on, then,' he said, opening the door. 'Help me with the tent.'

By the time the tent was up, the Place of Skulls was a bustle of activity as the men made preparations, but there was no laughing or joking. Instead there was a solemn atmosphere, and they spoke in hushed tones while Hamara directed them to do this job or that job.

Dad went to help Efra split huge pine logs and throw them on to a bonfire that blazed inside a circle of boulders. Others were putting up shelters, or rearranging their caravans, or lighting fire torches and putting them in the ground, even though it wouldn't be dark for another few hours.

It was spring, but we were so high up and so far north, above the Arctic Circle, that the air was still cold. The men were all wearing layers of sweaters and jackets that made them even bigger than usual. They looked hairy and ugly, and even though I saw them every day, this place gave them an unusual wildness, as if they had just stepped out of the forest. They carried rifles slung over their shoulders, and knives hung from their belts.

There were other boys there, too, all of them older

than me, but not by much. None of them spoke to me, though. Even my friends Jalmar and Onni didn't do much more than smile and nod whenever I caught their eye. Others, like Risto and Broki, looked at me and whispered, and drew their fingers across their throats.

I pulled on my woolly hat and went to the trailer, pretending to check the ATV. Dad and I had already looked over it before we left, so I knew it was in good working order and that all my gear was on the back, but I didn't know what else to do with the short time I had left. Soon, Hamara would call me in front of the men and all my fears would catch up with me.

As if to confirm my thoughts, the sudden crack of a gunshot filled the air. Sharp and loud, it made me jump, and I looked over at the platform as the shot echoed around the Place of Skulls and rang out across the mountain before fading into nothing.

Hamara was standing up there, looking down on us all, with his rifle in his right hand. He had rested the stock on his hip and the barrel was pointing up into the air. In his left hand he held a large hunting bow. He seemed even bigger now, like some kind of prehistoric forest animal.

Everyone stopped what they were doing and looked over at him as he fired off another shot. The rifle kicked against his hip, but he remained still.

When the sound of the second shot had died, Hamara bellowed one word: 'Oskari!'

My heart missed a beat and my insides tightened.

By the bonfire, Dad threw a last log on to the flames

19

and hurried over towards me, pointing at the ATV.

All the other men headed for the platform.

'Watch out for bears,' Davi said, slapping me hard on the back as he went past. He was Broki's dad and I hated him as much as I hated Broki. His slap knocked me off balance, pushing me into the ATV, so I had to put out my hands to stop myself from falling. When I turned, I saw Dad stop in front of him, axe in one hand.

'What?' Davi held out his arms. 'I was just wishing him luck, that's all.'

Dad stepped right up to him so they were toe to toe, looking into each other's eyes. His fist gripped the axe handle so tightly that his knuckles blossomed white.

'I'm all right, Dad,' I said, rubbing my hands on my trousers. 'Really.'

Dad's breathing became heavy and he continued to stare at Davi.

'You heard him,' Davi said, backing away. 'He's all right.'

Dad clenched his jaw and shook his head. I thought for a moment that he was going to hit Davi, but then another gunshot rang out and Hamara shouted once again:

'Oskari!'

'Better not keep everyone waiting,' Davi said with a smirk.

Dad swallowed his anger and stepped around him. 'Come on, son, let's get this off the trailer.'

He unclipped the tailgate, glancing back at Davi, who went to join the others around the platform. 'Don't worry about him,' he said. 'He's no one.'

So am I, I thought as I climbed on to the ATV and settled into the creaking seat. I felt small and afraid sitting there, and I imagined what it would be like to just drive away and leave all this behind.

'Come on, Oskari, hurry. They're waiting. And remember to do everything exactly the way I told you.'

'Yes, Dad.' I switched on the engine and throttled it before slowly reversing off the trailer.

'Quicker.'

I throttled it a little harder, and the ATV lurched backwards down the metal ramp. For a second I lost control, and sped off the trailer so that the wheels sank into a patch of rain-loosened soil and spun around, kicking up dirt in a dark spray behind us. I throttled the engine harder to get myself out, but the wheels only spun faster, digging deeper, and the engine revved loudly.

'God above, Oskari!' Dad leaned across to switch off the engine. 'How many times do I have to—' He stopped himself and closed his eyes, taking a deep breath. When he opened his eyes again, he looked at me. 'How many times do I have to tell you? If you overstress the engine, you'll damage it. And if you damage it, we'll have no ATV. We can't fix a blown engine and we can't afford to buy another one of these. Look after it, Oskari. Take care of it.'

'Sorry,' I said as I climbed off the ATV.

Dad sighed. 'It's okay. Just . . . just show 'em what you've got.' He managed a half-smile, then grabbed the handlebars, and together we pulled the vehicle out of the mud patch.

As we did it, I looked across the clearing where the skulls seemed to watch me from the tops of their posts.

You're going to fail, their dead voices whispered. *You're going to fail.*

The flaming torches surrounding the platform flickered in the breeze, and Hamara was still standing up there with his rifle against his hip and the bow in his hand, like he was waiting for his sacrifice to be brought to him. All the other men and boys had turned to see what Dad and I were doing. Some of them were laughing as I climbed back on to the ATV, but I gritted my teeth and ignored them. I tried to imagine they weren't there as I drove through the crowd towards the platform, the ATV rattling across the stones.

'Hey, Oskari!' Risto shouted. 'You might find some cranberries over by the swamp.'

'Or if you can't find any, just bring back some elk dung,' Broki shouted, earning himself a murmur of laughter.

'There's plenty of rabbit droppings!' another voice said.

I kept my eyes fixed ahead and pretended not to hear them. I tried to tell myself I would show them. I *tried* to tell myself that I had the map in my pocket, with Dad's secret hunting ground marked on it, and they would all have to eat their words when I came back with the biggest buck they had ever seen. Somehow, though, it didn't make me feel any braver or stronger.

Closer to the platform, I could see that the timber frame wasn't just filled with grey rocks. There were skulls in there, too, just like Jalmar and Onni had said. Hundreds and hundreds of them, most of them so brown and yellow they looked ancient. All those sharp, broken teeth and empty eye sockets, circled by the flickering torches, made the whole place feel like death.

When I was right in front of them, I stopped and switched off the engine, terrified by what was to come. I sat for a second, then dismounted the ATV, wondering how many skulls watched me as I climbed the rickety wooden ladder to stand on the platform beside Hamara.

I cast my eyes over the serious faces of the men below, hardly recognizing anyone because I couldn't concentrate on anything. My vision sparkled and blurred. My heart hammered in my chest.

Thump. Thump. Thump.

My stomach felt heavy and it churned like the time I'd eaten something bad and spent the whole night throwing up.

Then I caught a glimpse of my friend Jalmar, showing me a thumbs-up, and Dad giving me an encouraging nod, so I turned to Hamara.

Hamara stared down at me, fixing me with those cold eyes. For a long time, it seemed as if he wasn't going to do or say anything, but eventually he raised his left hand and offered me the traditional hunting bow.

I swallowed hard and reached out to take it, but he didn't let go. I looked at the bow, then at him, and tugged harder. Hamara narrowed his eyes and released his grip.

A murmur ran through the crowd below. Someone

23

mumbled something, and there was a ripple of laughter.

The bow was even bigger than Dad's. It was almost as long as me, so when I touched one end of it on the platform at my feet, the other end reached my chin. The wood was heavy and cold, but the grip was warm from Hamara's hand. This was the traditional hunting bow of our village, usually kept in the Hunting Lodge, used only for the Trial. It was ancient; the bow every boy had used to prove himself. People from our village had been hunting with it – becoming men – for more than a hundred years. My own dad had shot and killed a bear with this bow.

Now it was my turn to show what I could do.

All those hours of practising had led to this. All those days with aching arms and sore fingers, using bigger and stronger bows, had been about bringing me to this moment in time.

Be calm, I told myself. *Be calm*.

I closed my eyes for a moment, then turned to face the crowd and took up a strong stance, just like Dad had taught me. I held the bow tight in my left hand and took a deep breath as I raised it, hooking the fingers of my right hand around the braided string and beginning to pull.

The bow creaked and curved as it bent to my strength.

I kept my left arm straight and firm as I drew the string further and further.

It wasn't as hard as I had thought it would be. The hours of training had paid off. I was doing it. I was going to prove them all wrong. I would draw the bow all the way and—

Two fingers' width from my nose, the bow seemed to tighten and fight against me. The string refused to pull back any further. I gritted my teeth and summoned all the strength I had, but it just wouldn't budge. My arms began to burn. The sensation started in my forearms, then blazed right up towards my shoulders, and the bow began to shake. Panic threatened to overwhelm me. I couldn't do it. I couldn't draw the bow. I wasn't strong enough.

I glanced down and saw Dad looking up at me. He was touching the bear's tooth that hung around his neck, and there was an expression on his face somewhere between shame and pity, which only gave me more strength. I was determined not to let him down. I would show them all.

With a last surge of effort, I managed to draw the bow back another inch, so that it touched the tip of my nose . . . but no more. And that wasn't enough. It had to touch my cheek. The string had to touch my *cheek*.

That's when I knew I had failed.

Tears stung my eyes and I could hold the bow no longer. My muscles burned and my arms were shaking and my father hung his head in shame.

I allowed the string to relax and stood with the bow at my side.

Some of the boys in the crowd laughed quietly, but the men shifted in embarrassment. It was the worst thing that could happen – I wasn't even strong enough to draw the bow, how on earth would I survive the forest? And what would the forest offer a boy who couldn't draw the traditional bow?

Hamara took off his hat, crumpling it into his fist as he stared down at me. He shook his head once and turned to scan the crowd, looking at each man before his eyes finally came to rest on Dad's. Hamara watched him for a moment, then put out a hand and beckoned to him to join us on the platform.

Dad climbed up, followed by Siffonen and Rysty, two of the other senior men from our village. They were craggy and weather-beaten, like Hamara, with thick grey beards and drooping bags beneath their eyes. They approached Hamara without looking at me. It was as if I wasn't even there.

'What shall we do?' Hamara asked. 'No one has ever failed to draw the bow before.'

'The boy goes home.' Rysty's voice was gravelly from years of smoking, and his beard was tinged yellow with tobacco stains.

'The hell he will,' Dad said, standing firm. 'He needs to do this.'

'There have been exceptions.' Hamara looked down and ran a hand over his head. 'The Kuusisto boy didn't do the Trial.'

'He was in a wheelchair,' Dad said. 'He didn't even *try* to draw the bow. This is not the same thing.'

Hamara frowned. 'Maybe it's better this way. He's not strong enough. If he goes home, it will save him crying in front of the whole village.'

'Oskari does not cry,' Dad said. 'And sending him home will not save him the embarrassment.'

'Or you.' Hamara raised his eyes to meet Dad's.

Dad looked as if he wanted to hit Hamara. 'He's not going home,' he said. 'You have to give him a chance. We've been training like crazy for this. And don't forget who's teaching him. When I was his age I brought back a bear.'

'He's not you.'

'He's my *son*.'

The men fell silent for a moment, then turned to look at me.

I wiped my nose with my sleeve and stood straight.

Hamara shook his head again and let out a heavy sigh. 'I'm not going out looking for him tomorrow if he gets lost.'

'He won't get lost,' Dad said. 'He's smart. Just make your speech and send him on his way.'

Hamara continued to watch me for a moment, then he looked at Siffonen and Rysty, who shrugged. Hamara nodded and pulled his hat back on. 'Very well. Tradition is tradition.'

Dad spat into his hand and offered it to Hamara, who hesitated. For a second, I thought he was going to change his mind, then Hamara spat into his own palm and the two men shook once. The way they gripped each other's hands, it was as if they were trying to break bones.

When they were finished, Dad squeezed my shoulder then left the platform and went to join the other men. Siffonen and Rysty followed close behind, leaving me alone with Hamara once more. The crowd grew restless and muttered conversations broke out.

'Men!' Hamara shouted, bringing them to order. He waited for them to settle before continuing. 'This boy has the blood of hunters in his veins. He stands here as every one of you once stood. Ready to uphold our traditions. He has one night and one day to find out what kind of a man he is.' He looked sideways at me and cleared his throat. 'Tomorrow, he will bring us what the forest has seen fit to give him.'

'Elk dung,' someone whispered, making Hamara stop and scan the crowd with a frown.

'The forest is a harsh judge,' he went on, raising his voice. 'It gives each of us what we deserve. We must know how to listen, and fight tooth and nail for our prey.'

Hamara stood straight and lifted his chin with pride. 'This is what we have done for centuries and will do for centuries more. Nothing is given to us for free.' He paused and scanned the crowd once again. 'A boy sets out into the wilderness, but it is a man who will return.'

He put his hand on my shoulder and said, 'What do *you* deserve?' as he looked me in the eye and handed me a quiver full of arrows. Without waiting for an answer, he raised his rifle once more and fired into the air.

Immediately, the Place of Skulls was filled with the sound of gunshots as every man raised his weapon and fired.

Below, Dad nodded at me with the utmost seriousness. I returned the nod then, putting the bow across my back, I came down from the platform and climbed on to the

ATV without looking at anyone else. All I wanted to do now was get away from there. I wanted to leave them all behind. I wasn't afraid of going into the forest alone any more. I was desperate to go.

When I turned the key in the ignition, though, nothing happened. I swallowed hard and tried again. Still nothing. It was as if everything was against me. Even the ATV was trying to—

The engine roared into life and I throttled it hard. I took one last look at Dad, then put the ATV into gear and drove away from the Place of Skulls into the wilderness of Mount Akka.

My Trial had begun.

FIRST BLOOD

Best. Feeling. Ever.

The wind rushed in my face as I hurtled along the track. It was fantastic to be on my own at last. There was no one here to laugh at me, no one to let down but myself.

The trees were an emerald haze as they flashed past and I headed deeper and deeper into the forest, leaving the Place of Skulls far behind. The sun was falling below the treetops, the low light filtering through the pine needles, dusky and grey. The narrow dirt path that snaked up through the wilderness looked like it had been trampled for hundreds of years. Ancient tree roots broke its surface like the arching backs of sea monsters, and sharp rocks protruded here and there, but the ATV passed over all of it, bumping and sliding. I kept low, avoiding the branches that reached out across the path, and felt myself smiling as I rode on, the sound of the engine filling my ears, the ceremonial bow tight across my back. It really was so much larger than my own, but Dad had made me carry his when we had hunted together, so it didn't feel too strange to have it.

I had decided to head straight around and up the mountain towards the secret hunting ground Dad had told me about. From the look of the map, it was at least an hour and a half's drive from the Place of Skulls, followed by a half-hour trek on foot, but I reckoned I should be able to get there just before dark. Once I was there I would build a fire, and camp under the wind just below the place marked on the map. I had only one night and one day to hunt and bring my trophy out of the forest, so in the morning I would head out and try to find a buck.

I didn't dare think about what I would do if there was nothing there.

Glancing at my watch I was surprised to see I had already been driving for almost an hour, so I must have travelled twenty or thirty kilometres without even realizing it. I was making good time.

As I sped along the path, bumping up and down on the tree roots and rocks, I thought about what it would feel like to fire the arrow that would kill the buck. I imagined skinning it, taking its head and driving out of the forest with it strapped to my back, antlers spread wide above my shoulders. Hamara wouldn't look down on me then. He wouldn't be able to give me that pitying glance that said he knew I wasn't good enough. And, best of all, Dad would be proud. I knew that, deep down, he didn't think I was going to impress him, but he would be so pleased to see me bring out a trophy every bit as impressive as the one the forest had offered him.

Thinking about that reminded me of the photo I had taken from the board in the Hunting Lodge, so I slowed down and fumbled in my pocket to get it out. I rode with just one hand, holding the photo with the other, and glanced down at it.

Dad with the bear's head on his back.

He looked fierce in the picture. His face was streaked with dirt and blood, his mouth was tight, and he was staring right at the camera as if daring anyone to challenge him. I bet they didn't laugh at Dad when he stood up there on that platform the day before his thirteenth birthday.

I narrowed my eyes and clamped my teeth together, trying to imitate the look.

That's when a tree branch whipped across my face.

It was thin, and stung like mad, making me turn my head in one direction while the ATV went in the other. The vehicle skidded off the track, wheels spinning on fallen pine needles, and slipped sideways down a shallow ravine. The engine revved hard as I tried to stay on, dirt and loose stones spraying about me, then the ATV tipped completely, throwing me off.

I was airborne for a split second before landing on my side with a sharp jolt that clattered my teeth, making me bite my tongue. I skidded and rolled four or five metres down the ravine, bumping on tree stumps and rocks and roots as I went.

When I finally reached the bottom and stopped with a thump in the undergrowth, I opened my eyes to see the ATV, on its side, sliding down the dirt bank towards me. The bungee cords on the back had come loose and all my gear was spread across the forest floor, but that was the least of my problems. The vehicle was heavy and it was coming towards me quickly.

Without time to think, I spun on to my front and scrambled away on all fours, hands and knees sliding in the sticks and needles that covered the forest floor. It was almost like trying to crawl through slippery mud. Everything was happening in slow motion. Any moment now, the ATV was going to hit me and I would be crushed to death under its weight. Or left in the forest, trapped beneath it, with no one to rescue me.

Then my feet found purchase on a tree root and I gave one good push, throwing myself out of its path just as the ATV hit the bottom of the ravine and came to a stop, engine still idling.

For a moment, I lay on my stomach, face to the ground, breathing heavily and wondering if I was dead after all. I could taste blood and dirt, and grit crunched between my teeth. My muscles were too fired up with adrenaline for anything to really hurt much, but I was bleeding from a cut across one of my knuckles and my face stung. When I reached up to touch my cheek, my fingers came away with streaks of blood. I had the feeling that I would be covered in bruises by tomorrow.

Once I realized I was still alive, though, a thought popped into my head like an alarm bell.

The bow!

I could still feel the tightness of the string across my chest, but I got to my knees and slipped it over my head to check it hadn't snapped in the fall. If anything happened to the traditional bow, my life wouldn't be worth living. Hamara would be so angry if I broke it, I wouldn't be surprised if he cut off my head and stuck it on one of those stakes in the clearing.

I held my breath and checked the bow, running my hands along it, testing for cracks and weaknesses. I breathed out in a long rush when I realized it was all in one piece. There were a few nicks and scratches, but that was all.

There wasn't much time to feel relief, though, because the ATV was lying on its side, engine running, and Dad's words echoed in my head.

Look after it, Oskari. Take care of it.

We couldn't afford to buy another one.

I closed my eyes and made a promise that I would help Dad with the logs next week if only it would be all right. I said a quick prayer to the forest or whoever might be listening, then I got to my feet and sucked the blood from my knuckles as I hurried to the ATV.

With a great heave, I put all my weight behind the vehicle and managed to push it upright. I switched off the engine and checked it over for any damage. All around, the forest began to come back to life after the disturbance. Birds continued their late-afternoon song, and a woodpecker drilled at a tree close by.

Satisfied the ATV was intact, I wiped my face with my sleeve and set about collecting my gear and reattaching the bungee cords. I managed to find most of the arrows that had fallen from the quiver, so I replaced them and searched about for a good growth of moss at the base of the trees. When I saw a patch, growing thick and bright green between two exposed roots, I crouched and used my knife to lift it from the rich black soil. It came up in one piece, releasing a strong, earthy smell. Flicking away as much soil as I could from beneath it, I packed the spongy plant inside the quiver, keeping the arrows tight. They would be a little harder to take out, but at least they'd stay where they were supposed to. Slinging the quiver over my back, I returned to the ATV.

And that's when I saw it.

The buck was enormous. It was just standing there, behind a fallen tree, no more than ten metres away. It didn't seem to be bothered about me at all.

The animal's body was half hidden by the old, gnarled trunk of the tree, but its head and shoulders were clear. At least as tall as me, probably taller, the animal was fit and strong, its hide tight with muscle. Its head was turned in my direction so I could see its large brown eyes watching me, its ears alert as it listened to me, and its antlers spreading wide like a crown.

It was beautiful, perfect in every way, and it was mine. A buck, just like Mum had always said.

My whole body tingled with excitement. My heart

raced and my skin prickled. I had been in the trees for not much longer than an hour and already the forest had offered me a trophy. Maybe this wasn't going to be such a desperate hunt after all. If I killed this buck, I could return to the Place of Skulls right away. Imagine the look on Hamara's face *then*.

Without taking my eyes off the animal, I reached over my shoulder to take an arrow from the quiver.

The animal twitched and its ears swivelled.

I moved as slowly as I dared. The buck didn't know what I was and it was fixed to the spot, curious, but it might bolt at any moment. Its muscles were coiled tight now, ready to bound into action. I had to do this just right.

As I slipped the arrow from the quiver, I thought about how I would look in the photograph Hamara would take of me. Pale face streaked with dirt, dried blood on my hands. I would have the traditional bow in one fist, my knife in the other, and the head of the buck strapped to my back. Dad would be so proud when Hamara had to pin the photo up on the board for everyone to see what I had done; for them to see what kind of a man I was.

I nocked the arrow on to the string as the memory of standing on the platform crept into my mind. I saw myself failing to draw the bow, and for a moment I wished for my own. With my *own* bow I could . . . I gritted my teeth and pushed the thought away. I had to do this. I had to find the strength.

I took a deep breath and began to draw the bow.

A steady heart means a steady hand.

The buck continued to watch me, but his muscles seemed to relax. His ears twitched as if he was distracted by other sounds in the forest. He appeared to be losing his fear of me.

He knows you can't draw the bow.

I don't know where the voice came from; it just popped into my head.

I narrowed my eyes and tried to ignore it. I let my breath flood my body as Dad had taught me and I pulled the string harder.

The world became calm. There was nothing but me and the bow and the buck. Nothing else existed. I stopped hearing the birdsong and the woodpecker's constant drilling. Even the wind faded into nothing. The forest became silent, as if every creature was holding its breath, waiting to see what was going to happen.

The bow creaked a little as it bent. The string cut into my fingers. My muscles began to tremble. I released some of my breath, closed one eye and sighted along the arrow, feeling the excitement building in me.

The string was a fist's width from my nose when I couldn't pull it any further. My shoulders and arms were aching from the fall and now they were beginning to burn with the effort of drawing the bow. I was starting to shake, too, so I was losing my aim. I had to fire the arrow soon, otherwise I wouldn't shoot straight, but if I didn't draw it back further, the shot might not be strong enough at this distance.

I called on all my energy and pulled a little harder, but a distant sound broke the moment of calm. It started as a low rumble but quickly grew to a tremendous thundering beat, and then the whole world erupted into a whirling frenzy of sound and movement. It was as if a flash storm had fallen on the forest, bringing confusion and fear.

The noise was almost deafening. A heavy mechanical thumping that vibrated inside my head.

Thucka-thucka-thucka-thucka.

The treetops swayed in a whirlwind of movement, and the dry leaves and needles swirled on the forest floor as a powerful wind rushed among the pines.

Thucka-thucka-thucka-thucka.

The sound grew louder and louder as it came closer, and then it passed over in a deafening roar, sending the forest spinning about me.

The buck tensed for a second, then bolted, disappearing into the trees. When I looked up to catch a glimpse of the helicopter pass over, I twisted my ankle on a tree root and fell sideways, releasing the bowstring and sending the arrow shooting off into the air.

Tears of frustration stung my eyes and I yelled at the sky. 'Damn you!' I shook the bow at the sky. 'Damn you!'

I scrambled to my feet as the helicopter continued over the forest, skimming the treetops, and I saw brief snatches of the black-and-white paint flashing in the falling sun.

'Damn you!' I shouted again, hardly knowing how to deal with the anger and disappointment that ached in every fibre of my body. At that moment I hated that helicopter and everybody in it. I wished it would fall out of the sky and explode into a million pieces.

When it was about half a kilometre away, the helicopter stopped. I could just make it out in a gap through the treetops, hovering over the forest.

'Now what are you doing?'

It began to descend, disappearing from sight.

It was landing out there, and that made me even angrier. It had to be poachers. Here. In *our* wilderness.

'Patu,' I whispered.

Patu used to live in the village, but had moved to town and set up Safari Tours. He said he wanted to make money showing tourists the sights, but everyone was sure he brought men here to kill deer and bear for sport when he wasn't supposed to.

If it was him, and he was bringing poachers, then I wanted to know. That way, if I failed to come out of the forest with a trophy, at least I wouldn't be completely empty-handed. I would bring valuable information.

HAZAR

I knew I would have to go to the helicopter on foot, otherwise the poachers would hear me, so I hurried over to the ATV and grabbed my camouflage from the back. I had made it myself, using a large piece of netting and covering it with scraps of cloth in different shades of green. When Dad and I had gone into the forest to try it out, he'd spent ages trying to find me before eventually giving up. He said it was the best camouflage he'd ever seen.

I put it on over my jacket and hoodie and left the ATV behind, sneaking through the darkening forest. I moved almost in silence, walking on the pine needles where possible, or stepping on the tips of the stones that broke through the soil. The bow was snug on my back, the string tight against my chest, and the arrows motionless inside the quiver. I might not have been strong enough to draw the traditional bow, but at least I was aware of its size, and I was thankful again for Dad's insistence that I carry his when we were hunting. Not once did I snag the bow on the overhanging branches.

After a few minutes I came to a place where the trees thinned out and then, ahead, I saw what I was looking for. A large grassy meadow in a clearing on the side of the mountain, surrounded by the forest. It looked like a good place for deer, and I briefly wondered why it wasn't marked on Dad's map. I made a note to mark it myself when I got home.

The sky was grey and thunderclouds were gathering. The light was grainy and sparse among the trees, but still good enough to see out in the open. A distant rumble of thunder growled and the air seemed to grow even colder. Mum would have said that Ukko, the god of sky and thunder, was getting angry.

The helicopter was right in the centre of the meadow – engine off, lights on, blades slowing to a stop. The air shimmered around the exhaust, and the smell of fuel drifted towards me on the wind.

I crouched in the bracken below the trees at the edge of the meadow, using the shadow of a large spruce for extra cover. Close by, two plump magpies screeched a warning at me and hopped backwards and forwards on their branch. As they settled, I pulled my woolly hat right down over my brow, then scooped soil from the ground and put it into the palm of my left hand. I spat into it and mixed it into a paste that I smeared on my face, stinging the scratches on my cheeks.

I was invisible now.

Unblinking, I watched as the door on one side of the helicopter slid open and two men jumped down. Dressed in plain green combat trousers and jackets, with strong black boots, they didn't look much like hunters. More like soldiers of some kind.

One of them stayed by the open door of the helicopter like he was guarding something, while the other walked away and lifted a pair of binoculars to his eyes. I ducked down even further, sliding on to my stomach as he scanned the meadow, peering into the treeline.

Behind him, the pilot opened the cockpit door and stepped down on to the grass. He was about the same age as Dad, but shorter and not as strong-looking. He paused, taking something out of his pocket, then leaned back against the helicopter and lit a cigarette, watching the other men with interest. I recognized him right away. Patu.

'What are you looking for?' he called to the man with the binoculars, speaking in English. 'I already told you; I don't have a licence to bring hunters here. There are other places we need to go to for that.'

The air was quiet. The meadow was well protected on all sides and I was downwind of what little breeze there was, so his voice carried well and I caught a hint of tobacco smoke. I was surprised by what he said, though. Maybe everyone was wrong about him.

The man with the binoculars ignored him. He

continued to sweep the area, pausing when he was facing my direction. His body tensed and he stood straighter. He lowered the binoculars for a moment, squinting at almost the exact spot where I was lying.

I froze.

'See something?' Patu asked. 'Because the only thing you can do is look at it. I told you, I don't have—'

'Quiet!' said the man guarding the door.

'You can't talk to—'

'Quiet!' the man said again.

The two of them locked eyes for a long moment, then Patu backed down and lifted his cigarette to take a long drag. Before he could finish, though, the man who had spoken to him reached over and took it out of his mouth. He threw it down on to the grass and crushed it under his boot heel.

'What the hell is the matter with you?' Patu turned on the guard, standing straight and drawing himself up to his full height. Men from our village were tough and always ready to fight; he wouldn't like to be pushed around by an outsider.

'Relax,' the guard said. 'Stay quiet, do as you're told, and you'll get paid double.'

Patu hesitated, staring at the guard for a few seconds before moving away and lighting another cigarette.

The man with the binoculars took no notice of them and continued to watch the place where I was hiding.

I started to wonder if he could see me. Maybe my camouflage wasn't very good. Maybe Dad had just been humouring me. A surge of fear burned through my veins,

43

but I wasn't sure why. As far as I knew these men were just hunters, but something about them felt odd. The way they looked more like soldiers, and the way they spoke to Patu . . . it just didn't seem right.

Eventually, the man with the binoculars shook his head and went on scanning the rest of the treeline. I let out a long breath without even realizing I'd been holding it in.

When the man finally lowered the binoculars, he signalled to his friend, who retrieved something from inside the helicopter and came further into the meadow. He paused, then unfolded a chair that he set on the ground, pushing it hard to make the feet sink into the grass.

When that was done, a third man stepped down from the helicopter, and it was obvious, right away, that he was in charge. He was tall and fit-looking, with tanned skin and a neat black beard. He wore combat trousers, similar to the ones the other men were wearing, and a black leather jacket with matching gloves. There was an impressive knife hanging from his belt, and he was carrying a large case in his right hand.

He stood still and looked around, nodded at the two men, then strode out to the chair and paused before sitting down and putting the case on his lap.

Behind him, three more men climbed out of the helicopter and began unloading a number of aluminium crates. There must have been five or six of the boxes, one of which was almost as big as my ATV and probably just as heavy, judging by the way the men struggled. It seemed to be an awful lot of gear for a hunting expedition.

'Look, Hazar, if you want to stay here, it's going to be extra,' Patu said as he approached the man sitting in the chair. 'Maybe more than double.'

Hazar ignored him and smoothed his hands across the case on his lap before popping open the catches.

'I told you, this isn't a hunting area,' Patu went on. 'If I get caught doing this kind of thing, I'll lose my licence, and I got kids, you know. There are people relying on me, not to mention the bills I got to pay. You think running a bird like this is cheap?'

Hazar flipped open the case just as Patu stopped behind him.

'Whoa.' Patu was impressed. 'That's what I call a rifle. Is that for elephants? There's no elephants here, you know.'

Hazar didn't reply. He reached into the briefcase and took out what looked like the stock of a rifle.

'How much do you have to pay for a thing like that?' Patu asked.

Hazar took a second piece out of the briefcase and attached it to the first, clicking it into place.

'Okay, sir.' Patu held up his hands and started to back away. 'Tell you what, why don't I come back for you men later? I'll leave you here for a few hours and—' He turned around to see two of Hazar's men throwing camouflage netting over the helicopter, similar to the one I was wearing, but a lot bigger. Another two had opened the largest aluminium crate and removed a pair of long, fat metal tubes that looked a lot like rocket launchers I had seen in video games. But I had to be wrong. What on earth would hunters want with *rocket launchers*? I narrowed my eyes, wondering if I was seeing things, and watched in confusion as the men hefted the tubes on to their shoulders and pointed them at the sky. They swept them from right to left, then back again, before lowering them and nodding to Hazar. 'All good, sir.'

'What? Hey, wait a minute, what the hell's going on?' Patu spun around and spoke to Hazar. 'What the hell are they doing?'

'Don't worry about what they are doing. You should be far more concerned for yourself.' Hazar's words were icy and almost without emotion. He spoke English with an accent I hadn't heard before, and his voice was deep and commanding, carrying well in the darkening air. He removed another piece of the rifle from his case and fitted it into place.

'What's that supposed to mean?' Patu asked, and my scalp prickled as if something bad was going to happen.

'Well.' Hazar stopped what he was doing and shrugged. 'You should be running.'

'Running?'

Hazar stood and turned to him. 'I am a hunter.'

Patu looked confused and took a step back.

My mouth was dry and my mind was racing. Like Patu, I didn't understand what was happening, but I knew it wasn't good, and my fear for him was growing.

'I am about to shoot you.' Hazar's words were clear and unmistakable, but somehow didn't feel real. None of this could be happening. It had to be some sort of joke.

Hazar glanced around at his men before looking at

Patu once more. 'There really is nothing you can do to overpower me, but I don't yet have a complete gun in my hand, so . . . your best chance is to run.'

'What?' Patu shook his head and took a step back.

'You know how to run, don't you?' Hazar smiled, then pointed in my direction and waggled two fingers as if they were legs. 'I suggest you go now.' He reached down into the briefcase and took out the barrel of the rifle.

'What the hell is going on?' Patu glanced about in panic, now seeing the other men passing around sub-machine guns from one of the smaller crates.

Patu looked back at Hazar, as confused as I was. A thousand questions tumbled about in my head. Rocket launchers? Men who looked like soldiers? Sub-machine guns? And the weapon Hazar was putting together was nothing like any hunting rifle *I* had ever seen.

'Who . . . who are you people?' Patu stammered, and he stood for a second longer, before something seemed to click on inside him.

He turned and ran.

I wanted to do something to help him. I wanted to shout to him or . . . or *something*, but there was nothing I could do. Nothing at all. There were six men by the helicopter, all of them heavily armed, and I was certain they weren't hunters. If I so much as lifted my head, they might spot me, and then I would be in as much danger as Patu. The only thing I could do was stay hidden.

I could hear Patu's heavy, fearful breathing, and the thump of his boots on the grass as he came. I could see his eyes, open wide in fear.

I willed him to run faster, my whole body growing more tense.

Behind him, Hazar was working without any sense of haste, calmly fitting the barrel of his rifle into place, showing no expression as he fitted the scope and loaded the huge cartridges.

Patu was coming closer by the second. Almost at the treeline.

Keep running, I thought. *Keep running*.

Any moment now he would reach the safety of the forest.

Hazar snapped the rifle shut.

Almost there.

Hazar raised the rifle to his shoulder and sighted through the scope just as Patu reached the trees. He crashed into the undergrowth, sending the pair of magpies fluttering for deeper cover, and ducked behind the trunk of a thick pine. He bent double, heaving in and out, making wheezing, sucking noises as he tried to catch his breath.

Patu was so close to me I could almost have reached out and touched him. I looked up and saw the way his body shook in terror as he drew breath. I had never seen anyone so afraid before.

Out in the meadow, Hazar continued to sight along the barrel of his rifle, holding the weapon perfectly still. He was like a statue.

When Patu's breathing began to settle, he straightened up and smiled to himself, unable to believe that he had actually managed to get away. He shook his head and risked a peek around the tree at Hazar, catching sight of me lying in the undergrowth. At first he didn't know what he was seeing. A mess of green and brown, with two eyes looking up at him. Then it registered that he was seeing a person, and he opened his mouth to say something.

I lifted a finger to my lips, telling him to be quiet, but at that exact moment the tremendous *CRACK!* of a gunshot rang out from the meadow, and splinters of wood and bark exploded into the air around me. My instant reaction was to close my eyes and protect my head as the fragments peppered my face, stinging my cheeks and battering against my hand.

There was a sudden flurry of excitement in the forest as the wildlife dashed for cover, and a rain of pine needles scattered through the branches. Then the echoes of the gunshot receded, and everything became quiet once more.

When I opened my eyes, the tree that Patu had been hiding behind had a massive gouge right through one side of it, and Hazar was standing in the meadow, lowering his rifle, but there was no sign of Patu.

When I turned around, though, I saw him lying twisted in the undergrowth, shot through the head.

I didn't want to look, but I couldn't help it. The sight of him filled me with horror – his staring, dead eyes, the blood that ran from the wound – but for some reason I couldn't tear my eyes away. It was so unreal, like I was in a trance, or it was happening to someone else, or wasn't even happening at all.

Move! a voice screamed in my head. *Move!*

A surge of panic welled up inside me and snapped me out of the trance. It was like being suddenly woken from a nightmare and I scrambled backwards as fast as I could, breathless and desperate to get away. I pushed through the ferns until I was deep enough into the forest to risk getting to my feet, then I turned and ran for my life. My muscles were stiff from lying down for so long, but there was more than enough fear in me to get them moving.

I hardly even thought about what I was doing as I sprinted through the trees. All I wanted was to get to safety. Back to the Place of Skulls; back to my dad.

A DIFFICULT DECISION

I crashed through the wilderness like a frightened animal. Branches whipped at my face, and I ran with my hands up to protect it, not thinking about anything. All I could see was Patu's dead eyes.

My chest ached. It grew tighter and tighter the harder I ran. My muscles were numb, and I hardly even felt my feet as they took me closer and closer to where I had left the ATV.

Except, when I reached the place where I had slipped down the shallow ravine, the ATV was gone.

It was supposed to be right there, but it was gone. Either that or I'd come to the wrong place.

The light was fading. It was growing dark in the forest, and I had lost my way. It was the only explanation. I had been so desperate to escape Patu's dead, staring eyes that I hadn't paid attention to where I was going. I had just run and run.

I stopped and looked around, feeling a swell of panic. My breath came in small, painful gasps.

Or maybe they knew I was here. They had seen me. The men from the helicopter had somehow got ahead of me and taken the ATV so I couldn't escape.

Spinning about, I searched the area. It had to be here. *Please* let it be here.

Then I saw it through the trees just ahead, parked exactly where I had left it, and that awful feeling of dread faded just a little as I jogged towards the vehicle.

At least I had a way out.

Above, the sky grumbled and the first spots of sweet rain fell through the canopy of the trees. It was only a light drizzle, but the low, wild growl of thunder and the gathering blackness of the clouds suggested it was going to get a whole lot worse.

I was still breathing hard as I jumped on and started the engine, desperate to get away as fast as I could. When I looked up at the edge of the ravine, though, I realized that the bank I had tumbled down earlier was too steep to ride up. And I couldn't ride downhill from where I was, because a rocky outcrop blocked the way. The only thing for me to do was to steer the ATV further up the mountain and rejoin the path where the ravine levelled out.

The rain began to grow heavier, and the ATV's wheels spun and skidded on the damp soil as I drove. I tried not to think about Patu lying in the undergrowth, and the way that man, Hazar, had looked.

I tried to make myself think about other things, like: escape. And what were those tubes the men took out of the crate and held on their shoulders? Who was Hazar? And what was he doing in our wilderness? But no matter how hard I concentrated, I kept seeing Patu's dead body, all twisted, with his arms and legs in unnatural positions.

I shook my head to get rid of the image and made myself think about getting home. I concentrated on making it on to the path so I could steer back down the mountain and head towards the Place of Skulls.

It would be a long drive home, though. It had taken more than an hour to travel this far up the mountain, and it would soon be dark. At night I'd have to drive more slowly, especially in this rain, and it would take much longer to get back. Maybe four hours. Maybe more, depending on how long it took to rejoin the path. Maybe I would slip off the road again. Or, even worse, what if Hazar and his men heard my engine as I passed them on the way back? What if they came after me with their guns?

Just the thought of it made me shiver.

I pictured the map Dad had given me, and tried to think of another way back, but it was the red cross that seemed to call to me. The secret hunting ground. It was no more than a few kilometres from where I was now – a few *more* kilometres away from Hazar and what I had just seen. I was already heading in that direction and could find the path and be almost there before it was completely dark. I would be safely away from Hazar and his men. I could make camp for the night and then head back to the Place of Skulls at dawn, when the danger had passed. It made sense. I wouldn't return to the Place of Skulls as a man, carrying a buck on my back, but at least I would be alive.

Or maybe I would even find something when I was up there. Maybe I would see a buck in the morning, or something else. Anything would do. A grouse, or a rabbit, even.

Maybe I could take a trophy *and* tell them what had happened.

All these thoughts raced about in my head as I drove to the point where the ravine levelled out and met the path. When I reached it, I stopped the ATV and looked along the narrow dirt track that snaked down through the wilderness into the grey light. I turned my head to look up the path, knowing I could leave it a little further along and drive to the place marked on Dad's map. Then I looked down again and remembered what I had just seen.

Hunting ground or home?

Which way?

It was the thought of Hazar and his rifle that made the decision for me.

FIRESTORM

The wind rushed into my camouflage netting, billowing it out at both sides as I sped along the path, and the cold air prickled at my eyes so that tears streamed back into the edges of my woolly hat. The night curled around me, the rain hardened, and the sound of the ATV filled everything. It was like there was nothing else in the world except me and the terrible thoughts that spun in my head. But I had to forget those things. I had to concentrate on the task ahead of me. I had to get to safety.

When I'd travelled a little over a kilometre away from the helicopter – away from Hazar – I flicked on the headlights and followed the bright beams that cut into the falling darkness. Rain sparkled in the glow, driving straight down and pounding at my head and shoulders. It drummed against the ATV and hammered the path that would soon be a river of mud. The trees flashed past on either side, and my nostrils were filled with the sweet scent of pine and soil and decaying leaves.

An image of Patu tried to creep into my mind as I drove, dragging so many doubts with it. What if I was doing the wrong thing? Should I have risked passing the meadow? Should I have followed my first instinct and headed back to the Place of Skulls? What if—

WHOOSH!

My thoughts were interrupted by a tremendous noise from above that competed with the sound of the ATV's engine. I snatched my head up to look through a break in the treetops, just in time to see a white streak of vapour shooting up into the sky. It was followed by a second.

WHOOSH!

Then a third and fourth.

WHOOSH! WHOOSH!

They came from behind me, where the helicopter had been, like giant fireworks rocketing into the air, leaving long, white trails in their wake. I slowed the ATV and squinted against the rain, putting up a hand to protect my eyes as I watched the four lines slash out of view across the treetops. Several seconds later, the sky lit up in a blinding flash, followed by a distant boom and crack that fell across the wilderness as if I had ridden into the heart of a terrible thunderstorm.

But the light was too bright, and the sound was wrong. It didn't build up the way thunder usually did. It didn't roll and rumble and expand. It was too sudden. It had to be something else. Something to do with Hazar and those metal tubes I had seen.

Rocket launchers.

My suspicions were confirmed within a few seconds, when the sky lit up once again. This time, though, it was not a bright white light, but an orange, fiery glow. Dim at first, somewhere over to my right, but growing brighter. A sound accompanied it: a sort of rattling and screaming and growling all at once. It was as if some kind of monster was coming towards me over the wilderness, making the most awful sound that cut right through me, shredding my nerves.

The noise grew louder and louder, and the light grew brighter and brighter, then came the sound of ripping and tearing as whatever it was skimmed over the forest.

It came like a force of nature – like *Ajatar*, Mum's Devil of the Woods – breaking through the trees, falling lower and lower, smashing through the branches, tearing the trunks from the earth like they were nothing but twigs. The clamour of its approach was almost deafening. It drowned the sound of the ATV engine and my ears were filled with that screeching, ripping noise. It vibrated through me, shaking the ground like an earthquake.

There was a second when I thought I should do something – speed up or slow down or *something* – but that moment was snatched away when a huge ball of fire came smashing through the forest to my right, ploughing burning trees in front of it and throwing them out behind it. Sparks and flames exploded in the night as the object slammed into the dirt fifty metres away, sending tremors through the earth.

There was an ear-splitting *BOOM!* and fire erupted everywhere as the thing bounced and ripped across the track, gouging a huge tear in the ground and destroying everything in its path. It tumbled and barrelled, twisting and careering through the trees as it continued to my left, mowing through the pines and spruce as if they were grass.

All kinds of forest debris filled the hot air. Burning pine needles, incinerated twigs, smoking glowing leaves. Bark and wood splintered like shrapnel; thick tree branches whizzed like spears; pine cones popped and exploded like grenades. Before I knew what was happening, a huge juggernaut of a log came rolling out at me, slamming into the front of the ATV and throwing me over the handlebars, straight into the clouds of fire.

I sailed through the nightmare of black smoke and glowing embers as one thought went through my mind . . . *not again* . . . then a white light of pain flared in my head and I crashed down with a horrible crunch. I skidded and rolled across the forest floor like a rag doll, landing face down in a large puddle of dirty rainwater, while the firestorm raged around me.

SCAR

When I was five years old, Dad took me to the waterfall at Lake Tuonela. It was at least forty metres high and the water made the most amazing sound as it fell from the river, cascading into the chilly lake below. He took me to the top, right out on to a rocky ledge that hung over the drop, and we stood there looking down. I remembered how afraid I was to be so high, and to stare through the mist and spray at that angry, frothy water. It looked to me as if it was boiling, and I imagined the shape-shifter down there – the *näkki* – waiting to pull me in and drown me at the bottom. I had seen a picture in a book, of a giant squid trying to drag down a submarine, and that's what I thought of right then. I thought the *näkki* had turned into that squid and was looking up at me with those staring yellow eyes, its long tentacles swaying in the current, ready to wrap around me.

'Now that you are five years old,' Dad said, 'it's time for you to begin your journey as a man.'

I didn't have a clue what he was talking about.

'Don't be afraid, Oskari, you know how to swim. You swim better than I ever did at your age.'

I remembered looking up at him and nodding. 'I like swimming. Are we going swimming?'

Dad looked down at me with a serious expression. 'In a manner of speaking.'

I reached up to hold his hand, but he pulled away and turned to glance behind us. I looked back to see the other men standing on the rocks, Hamara right there at the front. He nodded at Dad, and Dad frowned and nodded back.

We stripped down to our shorts and stood shivering in the cold air, while Dad took a coiled rope from over his shoulder and tied one end around his waist. I asked what he was doing, but he just smiled and told me it was going to be fun. When he tied the other end of the rope around my waist, I finally understood.

We were going to jump.

'I don't want to do it,' I told him. 'Please. I don't want to.'

I cried and held on to his leg, my whole body shivering. I begged him not to make me do it; I was so afraid of that long drop into the mist and froth and the *näkki* waiting for me below. All I could think was that I would sink and sink and never come back up. I would never see Mum again.

Dad reached down and put a hand on my head to comfort me, but he was looking back at Hamara. 'Don't be afraid,' Dad said. 'I'll keep you safe. It'll be fun.' Breaking my grip, he pulled me away from his leg and moved us right to the edge. 'The rope will keep us together.'

Then he picked me up and stepped over the edge.

We fell and fell and fell.

I kept my eyes closed the whole way down. There was a tremendous tightness in my chest, pressing the air right out of my lungs as the wind rushed about me and the spray from the waterfall battered me like rain. When we finally hit the bubbling surface, there was a sudden sensation of cold, and my muscles stiffened as we cut through the water.

The power of the waterfall cascading above us was terrifying. It pushed us deeper and deeper into the never-ending darkness of the lake, as if we would never be able to get back to the surface. My lungs were empty and my head was pounding and I began to panic. I opened my mouth, desperate for air but sucking in only water, and right then, sinking in the raging lake, I thought I was going to die.

I thought the *näkki* had me in its twisting, crushing tentacles and would never let go.

That's what I woke up to now: the feeling of the world raging about me, a cramping in my chest and the sensation of my muscles tightening like cords. The memory of the lake was fading from my thoughts, pushed away by the sound of crashing and tearing, and the rain of forest wreckage that continued to fall on me. My face was right in a muddy puddle and I was drawing in water as I tried to breathe, but as reality snapped back to me and I remembered where I was, I lifted my head and coughed the puddle water from my mouth and nose. Lying on my front with my mouth open wide, I gasped for air, but something solid struck my back. Hard and painful, it thumped me right between the shoulders, and I immediately curled myself into a ball, tucking my head beneath my arms, wishing it would all stop.

I stayed like that for a long time, waiting for the worst of it to pass and for the terrible noises to die down. After a while, the forest grew quiet, so quiet that even the birds didn't dare sing, and the only sounds were the gentle patter of falling rain, the crackle of fire and the creaking of the trees.

Even then, I hardly dared move. But I knew I couldn't spend all night like that, so, preparing for the worst, I uncurled, opened my eyes and slowly got to my feet.

The path was gone. Nowhere to be seen. Instead, I found myself standing in what looked like a war zone.

A few metres ahead, there was a huge scar through the forest. That was the only word I could think of: *scar*. A massive trail of destruction cut right across what had once been the path, and now I was surrounded by broken and splintered tree trunks, scattered about like snapped matchsticks. Here and there, small fires crackled in the rain that now fell freely through the enormous hole left in the forest by the destruction.

Smoke drifted around the smashed trees. It settled across the ground or whipped about in storms where the breeze caught it and lifted it into miniature swirling tornadoes. The smell of it was strong, but it wasn't just the pleasant scent of wood smoke; there were other smells in there, too. Melted plastic, maybe, charred rubber, and even the cloying stink of burning fuel. And everywhere I looked, sparks and embers and glowing wisps of papery birch bark floated in the night, dancing in the dark like fireflies.

I stumbled about, shell-shocked, wondering at the awesome power of whatever had caused this, but also at how amazing everything looked. Despite the destruction, it was beautiful in a strange kind of way.

When I kicked something hard with the toe of my boot, I crouched to pick up a piece of steaming metal that hissed when the rain touched it. 'Ouch!' It burned the tip of my forefinger and thumb, so I withdrew quickly and pinched the cold lobe of my ear to prevent my fingers from blistering.

I booted the piece of metal away, and took the bow from my back to check it was intact. Satisfied it was in one piece, I ventured through the smoke, waving my hands in front of me, trying to clear the air. Stepping over small dying fires and broken branches, I finally found the ATV, upside down like a dead insect, with the trunk of a large pine lying across it. The vehicle was crushed beyond use. Three of the tyres were shredded and the front was dented.

Dad was going to kill me – if I even made it back alive.

I trudged over to the ATV and walked around it, wondering if there was any chance of saving it.

'Damn!' I kicked the side of it, making a hollow clanging sound. 'Damn!' I balled my hands into fists and put back my head and shouted at the sky. 'Damn!'

To my surprise, the sky answered with a blinking red light.

The strange red light hung in the darkness above the broken trees as if it was just floating there, and it took me a few moments to realize that it was actually growing larger. Whatever it was, it was coming closer, drifting slowly from right to left – the same way the destruction had come – and I craned my neck to watch it, mesmerized by the regular blinking of that red light.

On. Off. On. Off. On. Off.

'What the hell is that?' I whispered.

The light drifted lower and closer until it passed overhead and I could see there was something behind it.

A large dark shape.

I was beginning to wonder if the day could get any worse. First the helicopter and Hazar, then the . . . well, whatever it was that had just happened – some kind of crash or attack, I guessed. 'And now there's you,' I moaned at the blinking red light. 'What the hell are *you*?'

The red light didn't answer. It just blinked on and off and floated past, coming down in the trees on the other side of the scar. There was a crackle of breaking branches, followed by a soft thump.

Whatever it was, it had just landed. And it was close.

A part of me wanted to ignore it – to just keep on moving, but it had sparked my curiosity. I wanted to know what it was. And when I looked at the ATV, I knew I wasn't going anywhere in a hurry.

I glanced back across the scar. The red light wasn't far out of my way. In fact, it was more or less *on* my way. And it was probably my duty to find out what it was. It had crashed in our wilderness, after all.

I had to know.

'Right,' I said. 'Let's find out what you are.'

I jogged over to the ATV and salvaged what I could of my gear. The backpack carrying-frame was still intact, so I secured as much to it as I could and grabbed the bow.

Crossing the huge scar wasn't easy. I had to climb over and crawl under the fallen trunks of ancient, gnarled trees. The air stank of burning and it irritated my throat, making me cough when I was in the thickest of the smoke. I had to scramble through twisting clawing branches, all of them trying to snag my camouflage netting.

Despite the cold night air, I was sweating under my rain jacket when I finally made it to the other side of the scar and stood on a large, knotted trunk, watching the red light winking at me through the trees.

On. Off. On. Off. On. Off.

A shiver ran through me and I considered turning back. Maybe that was the best thing to do. As I stared at the light, though, I remembered Hamara's last words before I left: *A boy sets out into the wilderness, but it is a man who will return.*

A man. I should not be afraid.

'Be brave,' I whispered. 'Be brave.'

Taking a deep breath to steel myself, I jumped down from the tree and headed deeper into the forest, keeping my eyes fixed on the winking red light.

WHO ARE YOU?

Astrange metal pod was nestled at a slight angle among the ferns at the edge of an area where the trees were more thinned out. Shaped like a flat-topped cone, it wasn't much taller than me, and was shiny and smooth, like polished silver. There was an antenna sticking up from the top, with a flashing red light on the end of it, and two more lights on either side of the cone. They continued to blink. On. Off. On. Off.

An eerie mist had fallen with the darkness, and it mingled with the smoke from the fires and the firefly embers, so the red light washed into the night like smeared blood. Behind the strange metallic object, a parachute hung limp from the branches of a mountain ash, trailing along the forest floor. It was attached to the top of the pod by a number of cords that tightened and loosened as the material swelled and deflated in the breeze. At the front of the pod, facing me, there was a single door with a small window that glowed as if there was a light inside, but there was no sign of life.

Crouching at the base of a lichen-covered oak, I peered through the low branches, studying the pod and thinking that I had seen something like this before. On TV, maybe, or in a video game, I couldn't remember. It was like the kind of thing people used to come down from space, except they were supposed to land in water. I wondered if that was what it was: if it was supposed to have landed in Lake Tuonela but had missed.

But then I remembered the rocket launchers and the vapour trails and explosions, and I knew it had to be something to do with Hazar. The crash *must* have been something to do with him. But what had he shot down? Whatever had caused the scar must have been big and this was . . . what? Some kind of escape pod? Something *alien*?

The thought made my heart stop for a moment, but I told myself that couldn't be true. Why would aliens come to our wilderness? And was there even such a thing as aliens? Even so, I crouched lower and nocked an arrow to the bowstring, ready to fire at anything that might come out from the pod.

I waited for some time, expecting something to happen, but nothing did. The rain continued to fall, softening to a drizzle that pattered through the trees and gently drummed on the metal pod, and the red lights continued to blink. On. Off. On. Off.

After a few minutes, I lowered the bow and felt around for a good-sized rock. I inched closer, coming out from behind the tree branches, and hurled the rock as hard as I could.

Clunk!

It hit the pod with a hollow metallic sound.

Somewhere in the distance an owl hooted, but other than that, there was silence as the hollow sound echoed and faded into the night.

Without taking my eyes from the strange object, I reached down and felt about for something else. My fingers scrabbled about in the dirt before clasping another jagged stone, but before I could throw it, a bang came from the pod.

From *inside* the pod.

I scurried back behind the tree, peering around, half expecting an alien to explode out from the door.

Nothing.

After a few seconds I inched forwards, stopping to listen for a moment, then threw the rock. Almost immediately, another bang came from inside the pod.

Retreating to the cover of the tree once again, I collected two more stones and threw them one after the other in quick succession. They clattered through the branches and struck the metal object.

Clunk! Clunk!

The reply was immediate. Two solid bangs from inside.

Swallowing hard and toughening my nerves, I sneaked closer to the pod, walking carefully, making almost no sound. My steps were flat and soft, just like Dad had showed me.

When I was close enough, I stared into the steamed-up, glowing window and reached out, bunching my hand into a fist. Holding it close to the pod for a second, I took a deep breath and forced myself to knock on the door. The first time, it was weak and quiet, so I did it again, harder. The metal was sleek and smooth and cold under my knuckles.

A knock came from inside in response, and a dark shape moved across the window. I flinched and stepped back in surprise as the knocking continued. My instinct was to run, to get as far away from this thing as possible, but there was another noise from the pod; something like muffled shouting.

I stopped and peered closer to the misted window.

Once again, a dark shadow moved across it, then a hand appeared. It looked human, but I couldn't be sure – and I couldn't see what the hand belonged to.

It put out one finger and wrote something on the window.

1492

The symbols made no sense to me at all.

'Alien,' I whispered, hardly believing it.

Taking a step back, I tightened my fist around the handle of the bow and nocked the arrow back on to the string as I started to creep away. Whatever it was, alien or not, I would kill it if it tried to come after me.

In the window, the finger shook backwards and forwards a few times, exactly the way Mum's used to when she was telling me not to do something. When it stopped, it rubbed away the alien symbols and started to write something else.

1492

I stopped and stared as it dawned on me. They weren't symbols, they were *numbers*. 1492. The hand had written them back to front the first time.

Now the hand made a thumbs-up gesture before drawing an arrow pointing to the bottom right corner of the window. To make its point, the finger started jabbing in the same direction as the arrow.

Peering closer and looking carefully at the pod, I saw a panel just below and to the right of the window. It was a metallic keypad with numbers and letters printed on it.

'One-four-nine-two?' I whispered. 'That's the code?'

The finger continued to point.

'All right.' I took a deep breath and nodded. 'Be brave, Oskari, be brave.'

I stepped closer to the pod and put out a finger to punch the numbers into the pad.

1

I hesitated, doubt creeping into my mind.

4

What if I was doing the wrong thing?

9

What if there was something bad inside?

2

For a second nothing happened, then came a loud grinding of gears, accompanied by a clanking and hissing of hydraulics like someone had just opened a giant can of Coke. After everything having been almost silent, it was so sudden and so loud that it scared the life out of me. I jumped back and scurried into the trees, burying myself in a flurry of ferns and lifting the bow, ready to fire at whatever nightmare might appear from the pod.

The door popped open with a rush of air, and swung to one side, spilling orange light into the fine mist and smoke that hung in the air. It mingled with the red glow from the top of the pod, filling the darkness with colour that seeped out into the forest.

From where I was hiding, it was like watching everything through a greasy window, and I squinted, trying to see more clearly. It was difficult to make anything out, though, so I wasn't sure what I was looking at when a silhouette appeared in the doorway and unfolded itself from the pod.

There was a splash as it stepped into a large puddle that had formed by the door, and the creature grunted. This was followed by a sucking noise that might have been some kind of speech, or might have been a foot being pulled out of the soft mud.

The creature was nothing more than a dark shape outlined by orange-red light, but it looked more or less man-sized and man-shaped. I didn't want to take any risks, though, so I stayed where I was, crouching a little lower into the undergrowth.

With a sudden hiss, the pod door burst back into life, making the creature spin around with a start. It watched as the grinding gears started up again and the door returned into place and sealed shut. After that, the forest fell silent once more and the creature stepped forward, head turning. It stopped a few paces from the pod and lifted an arm as if it was looking for something, or reaching for a weapon.

'Morris?' it said. 'Morris?'

Was it speaking English? It sounded like English.

There was a sudden spark and hiss, and a bright blue flame burst alive in the night, dazzling me and making me look away.

'Morris?'

As my eyes grew accustomed to the brightness, I turned back to look at the figure standing by the pod, one hand held out in front of it, gripping the burning light that fizzled and spat like a signal flare. Smoke was rising from it, and the drizzle shimmered in its blue glow.

'Morris?' It spoke again and took a few more steps in my direction. 'Anyone?' Definitely English. Then the blue light sputtered and died, leaving the creature in the orange-red glow once more.

For a moment it stood there, nothing but a silhouette, then dropped to its knees and bent its head as if praying.

'Damn it.'

Whatever or *who*ever it was, it sounded lost and afraid. This wasn't just a landing; it was a *crash* landing, and one that might not be an accident. Something else occurred to me, too – if Hazar and his men had done this, then surely they would come looking. And how long would it be before they got here? I braced myself and rose up among the ferns.

Staying in the shadows, I drew the bowstring halfway, shaking as I tried to keep the oversized weapon steady while aiming the arrow straight at the alien creature. I took a breath, puffed out my chest and spoke in my deepest voice.

'Who are you?'

The creature stopped muttering and shifted, snatching its head up and looking around for the source of my voice.

'*What* are you?' I said, remaining hidden in the darkness outside the splash of orange-and-red light.

The creature moved again, turning in my direction.

'*Where are you from?*' I said, trying to sound older and stronger.

'Who is that?' the creature asked, getting to its feet with some effort.

I made myself stand my ground and hold the bow as steady as possible. 'I asked first. Where are you from? What are you?'

'What am I? What are you talking about?' It leaned forward, peering into the darkness.

'*Who are you?*' I repeated. 'You better tell me now, or I'll shoot.'

'Shoot?' The creature put its hands out to either side. 'No, don't. Please. I'm not—'

'How do you know how to speak English?' I demanded.

'I . . . um . . .' He peered closer and took a step towards my hiding place. 'Look, am I talking to a kid?'

I gripped the bow tighter and held back the string, wishing I could pull it further, wishing it was more deadly in my hands. 'I'm not a kid. Do you come in peace?' I asked. This creature didn't seem much like an alien to me, but that didn't mean it – he? – was harmless.

'Uh, yes,' it said. 'Yes, I come in peace.' The creature took another step forward, still holding its hands out to the side so I could see they were empty. 'And, um, I just want to point out, I'm not actually an alien or whatever else you think I am. I'm . . . well, I'm a man.'

I hesitated, feeling a little ridiculous but telling myself this was still a dangerous situation.

'In fact, I'm the leader of the free world.'

'What?' I plucked up all the strength and courage I had and stepped out of the undergrowth, holding the bow in front of me, pointing the arrow at the man's heart.

He must have heard me coming before he saw me, because he started backing away and stumbled on something, tripping and falling with a splash. He landed on his backside in a puddle, saying, 'Damn!'

Seeing that as an advantage, I strode closer so I was standing right over him, and aimed my arrow down at his chest.

'Whoa! Easy, kid.' He put his hands up in front of him. 'Come on, put that down. Please.'

'You call yourself the leader of the free world. What

do you mean by that?'

'Oh. Yeah.' The man shuffled away and got to his feet, so I took a step back. 'I guess it does sound a little presumptuous,' he said, drawing himself up to his full height.

Now that he was standing in front of me, it was pretty obvious he wasn't an alien, and I flushed at the foolishness of even thinking it. I could see now that he was tall and dark-skinned, and so bald that the orange and red lights glimmered on the top of his head. He was wearing a suit that was covered in mud and when I looked down, I noticed he was wearing only one shoe.

He followed my gaze, then looked up and forced a smile, showing a glint of white teeth. 'I know. I've got to admit, I'm not feeling too presidential at the moment.'

'You're a president?' I asked, lowering the bow slightly.

'Yeah.' He touched the lapel of his jacket, where some kind of badge winked in the coloured light. 'The President of the United States.'

'What?' I almost laughed. What on earth would the President of the United States be doing out here in the middle of nowhere? In *my* forest?

'Hard to believe, I know, but it's true.'

'Prove it.'

The man thought for a moment, tightening his lips. 'You don't recognize me? From the news, maybe?'

I shrugged. 'Maybe.'

'But you're not convinced, right?' He sighed and looked down at himself. 'Well, it *is* dark, and I guess not many people *would* recognize me in this mess. All right, well, I'm not used to having to ID myself, but . . .' He reached into his inside pocket, and I raised the bow once more, aiming directly at his heart.

'Whoa!' He stopped what he was doing and put out his hands again. 'It's all right, kid, take it easy. Just . . . look . . .' Very slowly, he pinched the lapel of his jacket with one hand and pulled it away from his chest so he could ease the other hand inside. 'I'm just getting some ID, okay? That's all.'

I watched him like a snake as he removed a small booklet from his inside pocket and held it up to show me before throwing it in my direction.

The booklet landed by my feet.

'You know my name,' he said. 'At least tell me you know the president's name.'

'Alan Moore. Everyone knows that.'

'Okay. Good.' He pointed at the booklet. 'Check it.'

'Don't try anything,' I said as I lowered the bow and bent down to take it. 'Stay where you are.' I picked it up and turned it towards the light.

A passport.

I glanced up at the man, then opened the passport.

There was a photograph of him inside, and it said that his name was Alan William Moore. I studied the photo, and looked over at the man. He ran a hand across his head as if he was smoothing down his hair, even though he didn't have any. Just like in the photo, and just like I had seen on TV.

There was no denying they were the same person.

'Do you always carry your passport with you?' I asked.

77

'When I'm going abroad I do. Everyone has to. Which begs the question: What country am I in?'

'Finland.' I stepped closer to him and held out the passport.

'Well, that's a start.' He took it and put it back into his jacket. 'Whereabouts in Finland?'

'Mount Akka.'

'We're on a mountain?'

'Yes.'

'And do you have a phone?'

I shook my head. 'Don't you?'

He patted his pockets, then wrapped his arms around himself and shrugged. 'I guess I left it on my desk. Is your house near here, then? A village or town?'

I shook my head again and looked him up and down, seeing the way he stood with his shoulders hunched. His clothes were wet through from the puddle and the rain, he sounded as if he was having trouble breathing, and he had only one shoe. He looked about as miserable a person as I had ever seen. President or not, he was a mess.

'Well, there must be something. I mean, where did *you* come from?'

'We can't go to my village now – it's too far and too dangerous.'

'Dangerous?'

'Yes. We need to go,' I said, remembering everything I had seen over the last few hours. 'It's not safe here.' I paused, hardly believing what was happening and what I was going to do. 'Follow me.'

He didn't move. He just watched me, and I knew he

was thinking the same thing as everybody else. Short and skinny, wrapped up in camouflage and with a backpack of odds and ends, I didn't look like much. How would someone like me be able to help someone like him?

'No,' he said. 'I'm . . . no. I have to wait for help.'

'*I'm* help,' I said. 'Follow me. We have to—'

'No offence, kid, but follow you where? You just said your village is too far.'

'Somewhere safe,' I told him. 'Somewhere we can make a shelter. A bit higher up the mountain there's a place. I can make a fire and—'

'No, we should wait here for help.' The president looked back at the escape pod. 'That's the best thing to do. There's a transponder in there, or whatever the hell they call it, and help will be on its way soon. Look, kid, you probably mean well and think you know what to do, but it's only a matter of time before this place is crawling with SEALs.'

'Seals?' I wasn't sure how seals were going to help us.

'Navy SEALs. Sea, Air and Land. Special Forces soldiers,' he explained. 'They'll be here any moment, so we should stay right here. I can't go walking halfway up a mountain with just one shoe.'

'So will your Navy SEALs get here before the men who shot you down?'

The president's mouth fell open and he blinked hard. 'What . . . what did you just say? Did you say "shot down"?'

'Yes. At least, I think—'

'No. No, that's wrong. We crashed. Some kind of malfunction and—'

'Shh!' I put a finger to my lips and stopped him. 'Listen.' I cocked my head to one side and cupped a hand behind my ear. 'You hear that?'

From somewhere in the distance, the faint but unmistakable sound of a helicopter came thudding out of the night.

BIG GAME

'**W**hat did I tell you?' The president sounded both relieved and excited. 'They're here to rescue me already.'

He turned around and leaned back to search the sky, but didn't have to look hard because, from the west, a helicopter was moving quickly over the forest, engines thumping. From beneath, a piercing white beam cut through the darkness and rain, illuminating the wilderness below.

'Over here!' The president ran to a gap in the trees and began waving his arms like a madman. 'Here! Help!'

The helicopter was already moving slowly along the burning scar, descending so that it was almost touching the tops of the trees. It was only a matter of time before it spotted us, but I wasn't so sure this helicopter was coming to rescue the president. This might be the one I had seen earlier, but this time piloted by Hazar instead of Patu. When I first saw the pod, I had wondered how long it would be before he came to find what he had shot down. *Not long* seemed to be the answer.

'Over here!' the president shouted again.

It would reach us in seconds. The noise was growing louder and louder. The treetops were swirling under its downdraught. And then it was so close it was deafening and the dry brown needles and fallen leaves were whipped up off the forest floor to swirl about in a hurricane with the embers and smoke from the fires. Grit battered my face and peppered my eyes. I shut them and turned away, trying to wipe them clean.

When I looked back, the president's jacket was flapping in the wind, the searchlight was moving closer, and clear as day I could see the words emblazoned across the side of the helicopter.

Safari Tours.

I stood in the middle of the hurricane as if my body didn't want to move.

The world swirled around me and an image of Patu flashed into my head. I saw him running in slow motion, I saw Hazar lifting the rifle. I saw the tree explode in a shower of splinters and Patu's body thrown away, shot and murdered.

'No!' I shouted. 'No! It's him!' I ran to the president, grabbed the back of his jacket and pulled, trying to drag him towards the trees.

'What the hell are you doing?' he yelled, snatching his jacket from my grasp.

'No!' I shouted again over the sound of the approaching helicopter. 'It's someone else, someone called Hazar. Please. You have to believe me. He's a killer.'

'A killer?' The president looked at me in confusion.

The helicopter was almost on us now. The light was flicking across the treetops, sweeping from side to side, and would soon be pointing right down at us. I kept seeing Hazar's gun and thinking that it was going to be pointing at us, trapped in that circle of white light.

'Please!' I said. 'Get into the trees! *Please!*'

The president glanced up at the helicopter, then back at me. He must have seen something in my face because he nodded. 'All right, kid. Go.'

We turned and ran, just as the beam passed close to the place where we had been standing. We hurried to the thickest trees and threw ourselves down into the undergrowth.

The president landed with a heavy thump as the beam flicked over us. The piercing light swept around, then quickly twitched back and focused on the metallic pod. The bright white light reflected from the shiny metal and lit up the forest. The dark shadows of tree trunks spiked out at all angles, so that now it really did look as if a UFO had landed. The air was a dust storm of clutter as the helicopter hovered right above the pod.

All around us, the ferns and saplings flowed and flickered in the current. The noise was deafening.

Beside me, the president started to get up, so I put a hand on his back and shook my head at him. 'Just wait,' I shouted. 'Let's see who it is.'

The president hesitated, still unsure.

'It's better to be safe,' I told him. 'Just watch. Please.'

He nodded and settled back into the ferns.

For a few seconds nothing happened, then the door slid open on the side of the helicopter and two ropes dropped down into the clearing, where they coiled like snakes. Four men, the ones I had seen earlier that evening, leaped from the helicopter and slipped down the ropes, two at a time. When they reached the ground, they unclipped and fanned out in different directions, crouching and aiming their sub-machine guns into the forest at different angles.

The president looked confused. These men were heavily armed and looked like soldiers, but I guessed he wasn't expecting his Navy SEALs to rappel down from a Safari Tours helicopter. He watched, open-mouthed, as two more men zipped down the ropes, landed and unclipped.

I recognized Hazar right away. He had his oversized rifle slung over his back and his black hair was shining in the light. He looked around, then raised a gloved hand to the pilot. In response, the ropes sucked back up into the helicopter, the doors slid shut and the machine turned in the air. It climbed high above the trees, then dipped its nose and flew away across the forest. The whole thing had taken no more than a minute.

When the helicopter was gone, there was a total

emptiness left in its wake. Everything was completely still and dark, and I didn't dare move in case someone heard us.

My eyes didn't need time to adjust to the darkness, though, because the men in the clearing were already emptying their backpacks and erecting tripods, topped with lights, which they aimed at the escape pod. I glanced at the president. He looked as if he didn't have a clue what was happening.

Close by, Hazar stood very still and scanned the area once more before looking at the man who had rappelled alongside him. The man responded by taking a strange-looking weapon from his back. He fiddled with it for a moment, then opened it up. I realized then that it was not a weapon but an umbrella, which he held over Hazar's head.

Hazar stayed where he was, watching his men fixing the lights and setting up what appeared to be a camera.

'What's going on?' the president whispered.

I nudged him and put a finger to my lips, shaking my head. Noise carried well in the forest at night, and we couldn't risk these men hearing us.

'Is the camera ready?' Hazar's accented voice was deep and he spoke slowly.

'Almost, sir,' replied the man who was preparing the camera, pointing it at the escape pod.

'What the hell is the camera for?' This voice made me jump. It was close, no more than five metres away from where we were lying, and whoever had spoken was in the forest; they hadn't come down from the helicopter.

Obviously Hazar wasn't expecting the voice, either, because his men whipped around and aimed their weapons towards the place where it had come from.

I pressed myself closer to the ground, making myself as invisible as possible, and nudged the president again, but he had already done the same thing.

'Who's that?' Hazar spoke quietly.

'Who do you think?' A figure came towards the other men, but was obscured from our view by the trunk of a large pine. It was impossible to get any idea of what he looked like, but he spoke with an American accent, like the president.

'Oh, it's you,' Hazar said. 'You don't look ready for your close-up; you're a mess. Have trouble getting here?'

'I did what I had to.'

'When you didn't show up, I thought maybe your parachute didn't open.'

'It did,' the man said. 'The others weren't so lucky. What's the camera for?'

'We're going to record this moment for posterity,' Hazar said. 'Big game hunting never got any bigger.'

'I'm camera shy,' the man replied.

Beside me, the president pushed himself up a little, as if listening intently while trying to see around the tree trunk.

I put out a hand to stop him but he ignored me and started to shuffle to one side, so I grabbed his arm and held him tight. The president stared at me with a grim expression. His eyes narrowed and his jaw bulged, but he nodded and eased back into the undergrowth.

'Are you ready?' Hazar asked.

'Yes, sir,' said the cameraman.

Hazar walked across the clearing to stand beside the pod. He reached out and touched it. The man with the umbrella followed him, keeping Hazar out of the drizzle.

'This is a wonderful moment.' Hazar closed his eyes. 'Something to savour.'

When his eyes flicked open again, they reflected the lights, making him look like some kind of forest demon. For a moment, I was reminded of Mum's stories.

'Tell me the code,' he said.

The man hidden by the tree cleared his throat. 'Fourteen-ninety-two.'

The president tensed beside me. His hands drew into fists and his whole body was shaking.

Hazar smiled. 'In fourteen hundred and ninety-two, Columbus sailed the ocean blue. Fourteen-ninety-two. Nice touch.' He turned and punched three numbers into the keypad.

'Gentlemen.' He looked back at his men. 'Prepare to meet the President of the United States of America.'

With a final flourish he keyed in the fourth number and a familiar grinding noise filled the night. It was followed by a long hiss of hydraulics, and as the door popped open and slid to one side, Hazar straightened up and looked into the pod.

'What the hell . . .?'

Silhouetted in the light, he stepped forward and paused with one hand on the edge of the door. 'What—' He leaned inside. 'Where—' He backed away in confusion, then whipped around to face the figure behind the tree. 'What the hell is this?'

'What do you mean?'

'He's not there,' Hazar growled.

'What do you mean "he's not there"? Where else would he be?'

'See for yourself.' There was menace in Hazar's voice as he moved to one side and pointed into the empty pod.

The figure hesitated, then came out from behind the tree and strode over to investigate. We could see him more clearly now – the dirty suit, a lot like the president's, and the muddy shoes that had once been shiny – but his back was to us, hiding his face.

'Turn around,' the president whispered beside me.

The man in the suit looked inside the pod. 'It doesn't make any sense. How the hell did he get out? I removed the handle inside. He couldn't open the door unless someone—'

Hazar pointed to one of his men, who came forward and drove the butt of his weapon into the suited man's back, just below his right shoulder. It came down with a hard crunch, and I heard the air go right out of him as he crumpled in a heap. He lay face down, then groaned and rolled over.

Two more of Hazar's soldiers came forward and stood over the man, casting shadows across his face as they aimed their weapons down at him.

'We had a deal.' Hazar ran a hand over his beard and spoke through his teeth. 'You promised to deliver the president.' He moved to stand over the suited man and exploded as if he couldn't contain his anger any more. 'NOW DO IT!'

'He's supposed to be in there,' said the man in the suit. 'I did everything exactly as I said I would.'

'Then how do you explain his absence?'

'Someone must have opened the door for him. It's the only explanation.'

'Out here?' Hazar looked about and spread his arms wide. 'In the middle of nowhere?'

'How about you let me get up and try to figure it out?'

Hazar considered the man's suggestion, then stepped back and ordered his soldiers to stand down. They lowered their weapons and the suited man got to his feet and began moving around the clearing, studying the ground. Hazar's men stuck close to him, blocking us from getting a good look at him.

'What are you doing?' Hazar asked.

'Looking for something. Anything.' He stopped and crouched, putting his fingers to the damp soil.

'What is it? What have you found?'

'A footprint.' The man stood up again. 'Someone *did* help him get out. Someone with a small shoe size.'

'Small shoe size? What does that mean?'

'Usually it means small feet.'

'Don't try to be clever with me.' Hazar snapped his fingers and one of his men sprang into action, raising his weapon. Before he could put it to his shoulder, though, the man in the suit whipped out a pistol as if from nowhere and fired two shots into the soldier's chest.

Gunfire echoed in the wilderness and the soldier

collapsed, but hadn't even hit the mud before the suited man was moving. He crossed the short distance to Hazar in an instant and grabbed hold of him, twisting his body so he was shielding himself from the other soldiers. He pressed the barrel of his pistol under Hazar's chin and spoke clearly.

'I've gone to a lot of trouble to organize this hunt for you, you over-privileged psychopath. Not because I wanted to, but because I need the very generous amount of money you're offering. I do not intend to lose that money because you can't control your temper or because my plans are ruined by someone with small feet. Do you understand?'

Hazar only nodded. His expression was surprisingly calm.

'If I'm going to collect that money, though, I need to deliver you the president – which I intend to do. Until then, you need to keep me alive, because without me, you will never have access to this' – with his left hand, he dug a phone from his pocket and held it up for Hazar to see – 'or to the information it can give us. And before you get any ideas, Hazar, this can't be accessed without my password. Now, do we have an understanding, or should I just kill you now?'

Hazar seemed impressed rather than angry at the suited man's outburst. He smiled and held out his hands. 'Fair enough. You argue a good point. So what does your useful telephone tell you? How long before the Americans figure out their mistakes?'

The man in the suit removed his pistol from under

Hazar's chin and stepped away, keeping the weapon pointed at Hazar's head.

'There really is no need for that,' Hazar said. 'You have my word.'

'For what *that's* worth.' The man slowly lowered his pistol, holding it by his side.

Hazar shrugged. 'How much time do we have?'

'Well, I disposed of the transponder, *as I said I would*, so right now they'll be looking for it somewhere over the Norwegian Sea. We have a good head start, and they won't think of looking anywhere near here until at least dawn tomorrow. No one is coming until then, so for now I suggest you call your helicopter back, because we're going to need the rest of your gear.' The man put away his weapon. 'Let's do what you came here for. We'll have a hunt.'

'Follow the small shoe prints?' Hazar asked.

The suited man nodded. 'Follow the small shoe prints.'

HUNTED

After seeing the man shoot one of Hazar's soldiers, and hearing what they were going to do, the president and I both knew we had to get out of there. Fast.

Staying on our stomachs, we slithered quickly and quietly through the undergrowth. Hazar was ordering his men to pack up the camera and lights, so their noise covered any sounds we made, and by the time Hazar took out his radio and called for the helicopter to return, we were on our feet and had begun our escape.

We hurried through the trees, putting as much distance between them and us as we could. Behind me, the president was breathing heavily and making enough noise to wake every animal in the forest. If he kept that up, those men wouldn't have any trouble finding us. They'd just have to follow the noise of his puffing and panting, and then we'd both be dead.

I didn't want to end up like Patu or the man in the clearing just now, and tears welled in my eyes as I ran. A desperation was building up in me: the sense that everything was lost, that I was going to die out here. I had come into the forest to find my trophy and I was going to die instead. I should have gone back when I saw Hazar shoot Patu. I should have returned to the Place of Skulls, but I had made the wrong decision and tomorrow Dad would come looking for me and he'd find nothing. No trace. Or maybe he'd find my body, lying dead among the fallen branches. Either way, he would be alone. He would have lost both Mum and me.

No. I stopped and looked back, waiting for the president to catch up. *No. I am not going to die.*

This wasn't about hunting any more. It wasn't about making Dad proud. It was about survival. It was about staying alive and not leaving Dad alone.

I am not going to fail.

'Stop,' I said, holding up a hand.

'What? No. We need to—'

'We're making too much noise,' I said. 'Leaving too many tracks.'

The president came to a halt and put his hands on his hips, looking back into the darkness. We had almost reached the place where the scar cut across what had once been the path.

'I don't see anything.' He was panting hard. 'We

'need to keep moving.'

'They will have lights,' I said. 'The helicopter has lights.'

'So what do you suggest? We can't stay here; you saw what they just did.'

I scanned the area, seeing the small fires still burning in places along the scar ahead. My mind was working clearly now that I had something to focus on. No more thinking about dying or hunting. All I had to concentrate on now was escape. That was all.

'We follow the scar,' I said. 'Everything's a mess already; they won't see our tracks.'

The president looked at me, a glint of fire sparkling in his eyes. He thought for a moment, then nodded. 'All right, kid. That sounds like a good idea.' He started to move, but I put a hand out.

'I'll go first,' I said. 'Put your feet where I put mine, and don't step in any mud.'

'That's going to be hard in this rain.'

'The rain is our friend now. It will help to cover our tracks.' I started to move but stopped again, the president bumping into me. 'Avoid the ash, too, and don't walk in the ferns. The leaves will drop and wilt, and if those men know how to track, they'll see it. Step on the fallen needles – the brown ones. And step lightly.'

'Anything else?' He put his foot down and there was an explosion of movement and sound from the undergrowth beside him. He jumped back in fear as a partridge burst out from the ferns and flew up with a clatter of wings.

I turned to stare at him. 'Yes. Keep quiet.'

I gripped the bow tight and moved carefully through the forest towards the scar. We crept through the last of the trees, keeping to the animal tracks and natural paths among the ferns, avoiding the puddles and soft mud. Coming to the scar, I climbed up on to the trunk of a fallen spruce and turned to see if the president needed help. He didn't seem like much of a woodsman to me, but I guessed he was more used to sitting in a warm office, getting people to do everything for him.

'Keep going,' he said. 'I'll be fine.' As he tried to pull himself up, though, his shoe slipped on the tree bark, and he only just managed to reach out and grab a branch in time to stop himself from falling.

'Come on,' I said. 'We haven't got time for this.'

The president said nothing. He just glared at me, then tried again, hauling himself up on to the tree trunk. Standing tall, he looked down at me as if to say, *See, I can do it*, and in that moment, I understood that we had something in common. Both of us had something to prove.

'All right, but we can't leave any trace, remember.' I crouched and reached down to wipe away the muddy smear where his foot had slipped.

'What the hell is going on?' the president said, gasping for breath as he looked along the scar, shaking his head at the splintered trees and patchy fires. 'What happened? One minute I'm in my plane on the way to—'

'I think those men shot you down. I tried to tell you that before.'

'But how? It doesn't make sense. Air Force One is

virtually indestructible.'

'Air Force One? That's the president's plane, right? *Your* plane?'

He nodded.

As we moved on, I told him everything I could: about the moment I first heard the helicopter, about Patu, about the rocket launchers and the streaks shooting up into the sky.

'Some kind of shoulder-mounted missile?' he said. 'They'd have to be powerful, though. Something high-tech and . . . wait a minute, we're on a mountain. They must have fired them from here so they'd be high enough to shoot Air Force One out of the sky. It's the only thing that makes sense. From down on the ground, they'd never have reached. But why didn't the countermeasures work? Why didn't the plane protect itself? Only way that would happen is if . . .' He went quiet.

'Do you know who they are?' I asked, remembering how the president had seemed interested in the suited man.

'Terrorists?'

'What about the one who came out of the forest? The man in the suit? He said he did something to the pod so you couldn't get out. How did he even know you'd *be* in the pod? How did he know you wouldn't just die in the plane? You sure you don't know him?'

The president stopped, but when I did the same and turned to look at him, he didn't seem to see me. He just stood there, lost in thought for a moment before he blinked and looked back into the forest.

I had a strong feeling there was something he wasn't telling me.

'I can't believe this is happening to me,' he said. 'Shot down, hunted, and climbing halfway up a damn mountain. And to make matters worse, I've only got one shoe and my foot is wet and it's killing me.'

I glanced down at his feet, seeing one black shoe that was now mostly brown, and one wet sock. I reached into my pocket and pulled out a plastic bag, then crouched at the president's feet and opened the bag. 'Put your foot in here.'

'What?'

'Put your foot in the bag.'

He wiped the rainwater from his face and sighed. 'I can't believe this is happening to me,' he said again as he stuck his foot in the bag.

I twisted it tight, wrapped the handles around his ankle and tied them together. 'There. Now you have a shoe.'

'Yeah. Kind of.' His face softened. 'Thanks, kid.'

'Oskari.'

'What?'

'My name is Oskari.'

'Oh, right. Oskari. Well, you can call me William. Or Bill.'

'Bill? Why not Alan?'

'I guess my mother preferred "Bill".'

'Bill.' I said the name again, testing the sound of it, but somehow it didn't feel right. 'No. I'll call you President. It's more interesting.'

'Yeah, I guess it is.' He put out his hand. 'Well, it's nice to meet you, Oskari. Thanks for coming to my rescue.'

I nodded and shook his hand. 'Welcome to Finland.'

His grip was firm, but not crushing, and when he let go, we stood facing each other while the drizzle fell on and around us.

'Come on,' I said. 'We need to keep going.'

'You're right. You first.'

I hurried along the tree trunk, arms out for balance, until I came close enough to jump across to a different tree. Moving like that, from tree to tree, we followed the scar for several hundred metres, passing small fires and steaming chunks of hot metal.

The drizzle was still coming down, but the clouds had parted in the distance, and the moon was shimmering over the mountain. On the scar, with no tree cover, there was just enough light to see. In the distance, though, the forest was black. That was where we had to go. Once we were in there, they would never find us.

'This must be where it came down,' the president said as we scurried along the fallen trees. His breathing was still heavy, as if he was having trouble sucking air into his lungs. 'My plane. Or one of the planes, anyway.'

'How many planes do you have?'

'A few.'

'Not any more,' I said.

The president made a sound that was something like a laugh, and I stopped once more to look back at him.

He stopped, too, and bent over with his hands on his hips. 'What the hell is wrong with me?' he asked. 'I mean, I know I'm not the fittest guy in the White House but, y'know, I thought I was fitter than this. When I get back I'm going to have to spend more time in the gym.'

'We're high up,' I said. 'The air is thin and you're not used to it.'

He nodded.

'Don't worry. I'll look after you.' It was unreal, like some kind of weird dream. Here I was, leading the President of the United States through the wilderness, trying to escape from crazed hunters, and I was beginning to realize that I was going to have to be the strong one. 'I'll keep you safe.'

'Well, kid, I gotta say, you seem to know what you're doing.'

'Oskari,' I said. 'Not "kid".'

'Yeah. Oskari.'

We continued along the scar, moving from tree to tree, leaving almost no trace that we had ever been there. The broken branches, the rain, the debris and the fires meant that it would be impossible to track us along this route. When we came to the end, we jumped down and jogged into the darkness of the forest that stretched out ahead as if it never ended. Only a small amount of moonlight made it through the canopy.

'Stop here.' I held up a hand, but the president bumped into me anyway, knocking me forwards.

'Sorry.'

'Pay attention,' I said, thinking how much I sounded like Dad.

'What are we stopping for?'

'We need to wait a few moments for our sight to get used to the dark. Let your eyes unfocus.'

'What?'

'Unfocus,' I said. 'Use your splatter vision.'

'My *what* vision?'

'Shh. Never mind.' I allowed my eyes to relax and not focus on anything. Dad said hunters had been using this trick for years, and it worked best in the open, but was good in the forest too. By focusing on nothing in particular, letting my vision go a little fuzzy, unusual movements seemed to jump out, demanding attention. I had used it to spot all sorts of animals, but now I was using it to look for a very different kind of animal. I was looking to see if there was anybody waiting for us, out there in the darkness.

Seeing nothing unexpected, I cupped my hand behind my ears and turned my head this way and that, scanning for sounds. An owl hooted, something scurried in the undergrowth . . . and there was something else.

'Helicopter's coming back,' I said.

'I can't hear anything.'

'Cup your hands behind your ears. You'll hear like a rabbit.'

'Really?' The president copied me and turned in the direction of the scar. 'I'll be damned.'

'We need to keep moving.' I scooped a handful of pine needles and decaying leaves from the ground and sprinkled them over the place where we had been standing, covering the marks we had left. 'And remember –

put your feet where I put mine.'

'Do you actually *know* where you're going?' he asked, glancing around at the forest, which I supposed looked all the same to him.

'Of course.'

So we moved on, deeper and deeper into the trees, walking for more than an hour, leaving the helicopter to sweep the wilderness in our wake as we headed up the mountainside towards the secret hunting ground marked on Dad's map. It was the best thing to do – the only place for us to go. When I didn't come out of the forest tomorrow, Dad and some of the other men would come looking for me, and that was where they would head. They would be armed, and they were expert woodsmen. Hazar's men might have automatic weapons, but I didn't rate their chances against a group of hunters like Dad.

'You need to be quieter,' I said. 'Walk carefully.'

'I'm doing my best.'

'Well, you sound like an elephant.'

'I'm not making *that* much—'

'Keep your feet flat. People think they should roll from heel to toe, but that's two points of contact and it's wrong. Everything you stand on will snap. An animal has only one point of contact and it moves like mist. You have to do the same. And try not to breathe so loud.' It felt strange to be in control for once, but it made me feel good, too. Like a man instead of a boy.

Behind us, the helicopter buzzed over the forest, its searchlight moving backwards and forwards. There would be men on the ground, following its instructions, and I wondered where Hazar was. Would he be in the forest, or riding in the helicopter with his rifle at the ready?

Mostly the helicopter moved around the forest behind us, skimming the treetops, but there was a moment when the thud of its rotors grew louder and it came zipping towards us, as if it had spotted something and was rushing over to investigate.

'Get down!'

We dived for cover, throwing ourselves into the dirt at the edge of a narrow stream.

'Over here,' I hissed, crawling towards the built-up wall of the bank. 'Slowly.' Any sudden movements would be much more visible.

The president followed me and we lay side by side and face down, squeezed into the side of the muddy wall.

'Don't look up at it,' I said. 'Our faces will reflect the light.'

'This is turning out to be a really crappy day,' the president muttered.

'For me, too,' I said.

We covered our faces as the helicopter hovered overhead, battering the treetops with its downdraught. The powerful beam of the searchlight flashed back and forth, cutting through the branches, glittering off the water and pouring over the rocks and undergrowth. The noise was tremendous, vibrating through my head and making my whole body tremble, but we remained completely still, as if we were part of the forest.

Eventually the helicopter moved on, but I decided we should wait a while before it was safe to continue our escape. We sat by the stream, listening to the musical tinkle of the water playing over the rocks.

'Makes me want to pee,' the president said.

'So pee,' I told him.

He stood up and went into the trees close by, making me feel the urge, so I did the same thing. When we were done, we washed our hands in the stream and set off again.

'We're lucky it's still spring,' I said as we walked. 'A few more weeks and the sun won't set at all. It would be much harder without the darkness.'

'The season of the midnight sun,' the president said.

'You know about it?'

'It's your summer, isn't it?'

'Kind of. We have three summers. Early summer, summer and late summer, except we call them Departure of Ice, Midnight Sun and Harvest Season.'

'That's kind of beautiful,' the president said.

'Is it?'

'You don't think so?'

'I never thought about it – it just makes it difficult to sleep.'

We changed direction from time to time, never travelling in a straight line. We backtracked and zigzagged and even used low branches to stay off the damp soil and confuse any tracks we might be leaving. Wherever I could, I stepped on rocks that jutted from the soil. Behind me, the president complained every time he put his bagged foot on one and felt the sharp edges bite at his skin.

Late in the night, we came out of the thickest part of the forest, moving higher up the mountain where the trees were thinner and the ground was harder and more uneven. This is where I would have had to leave the ATV before the final trek to the secret hunting ground.

'They could never track us here,' I said, climbing up on to a rocky shelf and turning to offer my hand. 'They won't even think we've come in this direction.'

The president looked at me. 'Up the mountain instead of down, you mean? You're a smart kid, Oskari.'

'We should be more or less safe.'

'More or less?' He declined my offer and hauled himself up, grunting with the effort.

'They have a helicopter,' I said.

The president managed to get one knee up on to the shelf but struggled to get any further, so I grabbed the back of his jacket and pulled hard. He half fell, half rolled on to the rocks and lay on his back for a moment, breathing hard. 'Helicopter. Yeah. Good point.'

When he was ready to go again, we travelled in silence for a while, both of us exhausted, and I cast my mind back over everything that had happened.

'What is Morris?' I asked. 'You were saying it when you came out of the pod. Is it a person?'

'Morris is my personal bodyguard.' The president was still breathing heavily, but not as much as before. 'He's saved my life more than once.'

'He must be very brave. Is he a hunter?' We entered a

small brake of scrawny pines and I held back a whip-like branch, waiting for the president to follow.

'Not really.' He nodded thanks. 'Morris puts himself in harm's way for me, though.'

'What does that mean?'

He stopped just inside the trees and put his hands on his hips. 'Well, it means that when I was in Seattle and made the mistake of deciding to meet-and-greet a crowd, and someone came at me with a gun, Morris was the man who stepped in the way. He was shot right here.' The president tapped his chest. 'Still has a fragment of the bullet this close to his heart.' He held his forefinger and thumb less than two centimetres apart. 'It was too dangerous to remove it, they said, but apparently one day it will work its way right into his heart and kill him.'

'So it's like he's already dead?' I asked, turning to look at him.

'In a way. I wanted him to retire but he wouldn't listen. Maybe it's just as well – he's the one who saved me by getting me to the pod before . . .' His voice trailed away and he stopped as if something had occurred to him.

'What is it?'

He put a hand to his mouth and stared at the ground. 'President?'

He looked up. 'Hmm?' There was a distant look in his eyes, like he was seeing right through me. It was the same as before, when I'd asked him about the man in the suit. 'Oh. Nothing. Nothing.' He shook his head and continued walking. When he spoke again, though, there was still a hint of something in his voice, and it seemed to me that his mind was somewhere else. 'Anyway, one good thing about being president is that I know the greatest resources on the planet are being disposed to facilitate my rescue.'

'What does *that* mean?' I asked.

'It means that a lot of people will be looking for me.'

'In the wrong place.'

'Hmm?'

'The man in the suit said he got rid of your . . . what did you call it? The signal thing.'

'Transponder.'

'Yes. So everyone will be looking in the wrong place.'

'They'll realize soon enough,' the president said. 'Then they'll come looking here.'

'But not until dawn. At least, that's what the man said.'

'I know what he said.' The president sounded annoyed. 'I heard him, too.'

'Well, then I guess it's good I found you. I mean, if I hadn't, those men would have you now. And even if you *had* got out of the pod, you'd have no chance of survival out here without me. I understand the wilderness; it's my home.' I felt a small sense of pride. 'With this bow, I can catch us food and keep us safe. And there are bears in these mountains,' I told him. 'I'll keep you safe from them, too.'

'There are bears here?' He sounded worried and looked around us.

'Many.'

'And you could kill one with that bow you're carrying?' There was doubt in his voice.

'Of course. This is a very powerful bow.'

'Have you done it before?'

'Yes. Well – no. But my dad has. When he was exactly the same age as me.' I put a hand in my pocket and felt the photograph between my fingers.

'And how old *are* you?'

'Twelve,' I said. 'Thirteen tomorrow.'

'Wow. Okay. My son is thirteen,' the president said. 'I have a daughter, too. She's eleven.'

'What does your son like to hunt?'

The president laughed. 'Umm . . . we don't really hunt.'

'You don't hunt?' I looked back at him with suspicion.

He shrugged and shook his head.

'Well, the brown bear is the most sacred animal,' I said. 'So after Dad killed it, they had a huge feast in its honour so its spirit wouldn't be angry, and then its skull was put on the highest pine pole so its spirit could enter the heavens.'

'Your dad sounds like quite a guy. I guess you want to be just like him, right?'

'He has taught me everything he knows.'

'Does that include telling you about a safe place somewhere out here?'

'Yes. We're going to Dad's secret hunting ground. We'll be safe there.'

But with the helicopter and all those men searching the forest, I couldn't stop the doubt from creeping in.

DEATH ON THE MOUNTAIN

Out of the main forest around the lower part of Mount Akka, and further up where the terrain was more rugged and the trees were thinner, I stopped to scan our surroundings. I let my eyes unfocus so I would notice any unusual movements, but there was nothing behind us. When I turned to watch the mountain ridge in front of us, though, I saw a rabbit hop once, then stop to look about. It was a perfect silhouette, exactly the same shape as the targets Dad made for practice.

I signalled to the president to stop, then lifted the bow and quietly nocked an arrow. I raised, aimed and drew back the string. As soon as I started to pull it back, though, I began to feel angry. The bow was too big and too strong for me. It was almost useless and made me feel weak. I gritted my teeth and pulled with all my strength, but as before, I couldn't get the string to my cheek.

I fired anyway.

The string twanged and the arrow skewed as it left the bow. It flew in an awkward curve, bouncing off the rocks to the left of the rabbit.

The rabbit didn't waste any time making its getaway. One moment it was there, and the next it was gone.

'Tough break,' the president whispered, but I ignored him.

Annoyed and embarrassed, I lowered the bow and went to retrieve my arrow, slipping it into the quiver and looking back, seeing the forest behind us. We had climbed a long way, so now the thickest trees were below, and I could see the helicopter sweeping the forest. It wasn't much more than a small red light, with a beam of white piercing down from it.

I shifted my gaze and looked at the president. 'If I had a smaller bow, my *own* bow, I would have hit it. We could've had rabbit for dinner if this stupid bow wasn't so big.'

'It's all right,' he said. 'We'll just have to go without dinner tonight.' He started walking towards me, stepping from boulder to boulder. 'Besides, I'm not a big fan of rabbit. I prefer a cheeseburger.' He stopped and looked down between two large, jagged rocks. 'What's this?' The president squatted and reached down to grab whatever it was that he had seen. 'A shoe,' he said, holding it up.

'Yours?' I asked. There was enough moonlight for me to see that it was a black, shiny shoe, the kind a president might wear. It certainly wasn't a hunter's boot, and I'd never seen anyone in my village wear anything like it.

'Not mine.' He shook his head and let his hand drop to his side.

'Is it your size, then? Maybe it's your lucky day.'

'Not *that* lucky. It looks about the right size, but it's the wrong foot.'

'Oh.' I looked around, wondering where it might have come from, and spotted something sticking out from a rocky ledge at head height about a metre to my right.

'Stay where you are,' the president said.

'What?' I was surprised. Since leaving the site of the escape pod, I had been giving all the orders, because this was *my* forest and he was the stranger. I didn't understand why he suddenly thought *he* should be giving them. But then, he was an adult, and adults always thought they knew best – probably even more so when they were the President of the United States.

'I said "Stay where you are".' He put a hand on my arm and walked past, going to the rocky ledge and looking up. He stood there for a moment, then began to climb. When he put his hand on the top, ready to pull himself up, he snatched it back and looked at his fingers.

'What is it?' I asked.

'Just stay there.' He got a good grip on the rocks and hauled himself up, making a better job of it than he

110

had earlier.

For a few seconds he said nothing. All I could hear was the wind and the distant thumping of the helicopter. Then the president spoke.

'Otis. Oh, God, no.'

I watched him, deciding that he wasn't in charge here. This was my forest and I knew it better than he did, so I hopped across the boulders and climbed up the rocks to see what he had found.

The dead man was wearing a suit, just like the man who had appeared from the trees where the pod had come down. He was lying face up on the rocky outcrop, with one shoeless foot sticking out over the edge. He was twisted in an awkward way, so his arms were in strange positions, and one leg was tucked underneath him, but his face just looked like he had fallen asleep with his eyes open. There wasn't a scratch on it.

I knew he was dead, just like Patu and just like the man by the escape pod.

'You know him?' I heard myself ask.

The president was crouched beside the body, with one fist to his mouth as if to keep calm. He swallowed hard. 'Otis. Part of my guard detail.'

'Bodyguards, you mean?' I took a deep breath and looked out across the ledge, where other dark shapes were splayed on the rocks.

The president nodded.

'And there are others, right?'

'Yes.'

'Is it them?' I raised my arm and pointed.

The president turned to follow the line of my finger. He stared for a moment, then stood and went to look at the other bodies. I stayed where I was. I didn't want to see any more dead people.

'Stanley,' he said looking at the first man. 'And Clay,' he said when he came to the other. His voice was quiet and sounded like it was breaking. He stood with his head lowered and his hands on his face. 'What happened to them?'

The president came back to me and rolled Otis on to his front to reveal the unopened parachute strapped to the man's back. He crouched and looked at the fastenings.

'Oh, God,' he said.

'What is it?'

'Oh, my God.'

'What is it?' I asked again. 'Tell me, President.'

He sat back and shook his head. 'Cable-tied. Some-one has tied the parachute shut. They were murdered.'

'What? By who?' Even as I said it, though, I remembered the man in the suit saying something about the others not being *so lucky*.

'The same people who are after me, I guess.'

'But you don't know who they are? Are you sure you didn't recognize any of them? They said they were *hunting* you.'

The president didn't look at me. He turned away and bit his bottom lip as if there was something more than our situation on his mind.

'What about that man Hazar?' I asked. 'You know him?'

He shook his head.

'The others, then? Did you—'

'I'm the President of the United States, Oskari; there are a lot of people who would like to kill me.'

A terrible shiver ran through me, like spiders crawling over my skin, but I told myself that standing around feeling sorry for myself wasn't going to get anything done. *Crying never helped anyone* is what Dad would have said.

'Get up, President.'

'Hmm?'

'I said "Get up".'

The president shook his head. 'They were murdered, Oskari, don't you understand? I've been betrayed. Someone sabotaged Air Force One so that it could be shot down, then they sabotaged my bodyguards' parachutes. They sabotaged the escape pod, too; that's why I couldn't open the door.'

'I know. I heard the man in the suit say that.'

The president looked up at me. 'You know that help I told you about? I'm not so sure it's going to come.'

'Stop feeling sorry for yourself.' I could hardly believe I was saying it, but I could see the president was losing heart. I had to try to keep him going. 'Stand up and let's go.'

'They have guns, Oskari. They have a *helicopter*. And they've got information, too. I mean, how the hell did they do all this?'

I looked down at Otis's body. 'Does *he* have a gun?'

'Hmm?'

'This bodyguard. He has a gun?'

The president seemed to realize what I was saying. 'Yes. Yes, he does.' He shifted and took a deep breath before reaching inside the man's jacket and pulling out a pistol.

'Now *you* have a gun,' I said. 'And I have my bow.'

The president didn't look too impressed by that, and after my performance with the rabbit I could hardly blame him. He tried to smile, but it just looked desperate, as if he felt sorry for me and knew we were already dead. Then his face fell as something else occurred to him.

'Phones,' he said. 'They'll have phones.' He dropped into a crouch once more and, with some effort, rolled the body on to its back. He turned his head as he patted Otis's clothes, not wanting to look at his bodyguard's face. When he came to the hip pocket, he stopped and looked at me with an air of triumph. 'That's what I'm talking about,' he said, fumbling his hand into Otis's pocket to retrieve the mobile phone. He lifted it towards the moonlight and turned it around in his hands, pressing buttons, becoming more and more agitated. 'Damn it. Broken.'

He threw it out on to the rocks and went to the next bodyguard, checking his pockets until he found another broken phone. 'One more try,' he said to himself. 'One more chance.' When the third phone lit up in his hands, he looked like a child. His whole face became one big smile and I felt so happy for him. He really seemed to think that the phone would save his life. He could phone for help, and we would be rescued.

But his happiness did not last long. He began to shake the phone. He turned around. He held it up to the sky. He lowered it. He held it at arm's length, then began jumping from boulder to boulder. Eventually, the air went out of him and his whole body sagged.

'What is it, President?'

'No signal,' he said. 'After all that, there's no damn signal.'

'Well, we *are* in the wilderness. I thought maybe the president's phones might work, but . . .' I shrugged.

He put the phone in his pocket and sat down, rubbing his face with his hands. 'Being the president doesn't count for much out here in the wilderness, I guess.'

'Not really.'

'Out here, I'm just like everyone else.'

'Maybe not even that,' I said.

'Thanks, kid.'

'Well, can you hunt?'

'No.' He seemed to shrink under the weight of our situation.

'Build a shelter?'

He shook his head.

'Can you even start a fire?' I asked.

'No.'

'Then you really *are* lucky I found you. I know how to do all those things. And tomorrow this forest will be full of hunters from my village, and the first place they will go to is my dad's hunting ground. That's where he'll come looking for me if I don't return by tomorrow.'

'Tomorrow might be too late.' He looked back at the helicopter sweeping the forest. 'Who the hell is doing this?'

'The helicopter won't do them any good. They're looking in the wrong place. Because you have me.'

The president sighed.

'If it wasn't for me, Hazar would have you by now.' It was a good feeling to think that maybe I wasn't such a bad woodsman after all. 'Haven't I already got you this far?' I asked.

He nodded. 'I guess you have, kid.'

'I told you, my name is Oskari. I'm not a kid.'

'No. I guess you're not.'

'Don't worry, President. I am going to look after you, okay?' I spat in my hand and held it out to him.

The president looked at me, then at my hand.

'Spit and shake,' I said.

He hesitated, then spat in his palm and grasped my hand. When he did, I gripped it as hard as I could and pulled, making him get to his feet. 'There,' I said. 'It is a promise now.'

The president gave me a look that made me feel proud and strong like never before. A sparkle came back into his eyes and I could see it was the look of a man who had chosen not to give up. Maybe he thought that if I could be brave, then he should be brave too.

'Thank you,' he said.

'Good.' I let go of his hand and shifted the pack on my back, then started up the mountain once more. As I walked, I looked over my shoulder. 'Oh, and you know why else you're lucky?'

'Why's that?'

I nodded at Otis. 'Right size, remember? At least his other shoe will fit you.'

FROM THE
SAME WOOD

Higher up the mountain, about twenty minutes after finding the bodies, the constant helicopter sound changed and we turned to see its lights descending into the trees below. For a moment the noise lulled, then it stopped completely. The president and I stood together, watching the quiet forest, wondering what Hazar and his men were up to.

'Conserving fuel,' the president said. 'They can't keep that thing in the air all night.'

'They'll start again when it's light. Or maybe they've decided just to track us on foot.'

The president turned to look at me. 'Could they do

that? D'you think they've found a trail? Is that why they've landed the chopper?' There was fear in his voice. 'They know where we are?'

'Impossible.' I thought back to everything we had done to cover our tracks. Not even Dad would have been able to follow us. 'We didn't leave a trail.'

'Fuel, then,' the president said.

'Fuel,' I agreed.

We stayed as we were, looking out at the wilderness, a sea of black stretching as far as the horizon, where it met the dark-blue sky. Stars glittered in and out of the passing clouds. From this high up we could see two scars, some distance apart, glowing like ugly wounds in the forest's body. The flames were still burning, illuminating the destruction that cut through the trees for at least half a kilometre, ending with large fires like full stops at the ends of sentences.

'Those must be the two escort fighters,' the president said. 'Or what's left of them. They're both too small to be Air Force One.'

'I wonder where that is, then. I can't see any other planes.'

He didn't say anything, he just shook his head, and we stared at the fires for a while longer before setting off again.

The president checked his phone from time to time, but always with the same disappointing result.

The air was colder the higher we went, and he was shivering. His clothes were damp from the rain, and his breathing was becoming laboured again. He needed warmth and rest, and we were both tired, but we pushed on. We scrambled over loose rocks, trekked through thinning patches of pines, climbed ledges and boulders. And all the time, we tried to leave no trace that we had ever been there.

When we finally reached an open, rocky plateau on the side of Mount Akka, close to the secret hunting ground marked on Dad's map, I stopped and went to the sheer edge at the side of the mountain, to look out across the wilderness. The chilly wind whistled about me, plucking at my camouflage and snaking under my rain jacket. I watched the flickering scars in the forest far below, then looked back at the way we had climbed before I turned to inspect the rest of the plateau.

The ground here was mostly bare and hard, but there were areas of grass, and the occasional spindly tree trying to live in patches of thin soil. On one side – the side opposite the way we had climbed up – the plateau sloped gently around the side of Mount Akka towards Dad's secret hunting ground. On the other side, opposite the sheer drop off into the forest, the crags of Mount Akka rose steeply towards the summit, but there was a large overhang in the rocks that would provide a good shelter.

Dad had told me to wait until dawn and stay under the wind, and even though I wasn't going to be doing much hunting right now, I glanced up to check the sky.

The president came to stand beside me and looked up. The sky was more or less clear above us now, and the moon was a large silver disc, with just a few clouds passing across it. From time to time, they dulled the silvery light.

'See the way the clouds are moving?' I said. 'The wind is blowing across the mountain. It means we're under the wind from above and below.'

'And that means . . .?'

'It means we can have a small fire and the smoke won't blow down the mountain to . . .' I glanced back at the trees below us. 'To them.' The helicopter was gone now, but we knew the men might be down there, maybe searching the forest on foot.

I told the president to sit under the overhang and shelter out of the wind while I prepared a fire. There weren't many trees around the plateau, but there were enough for me to gather wood to last for a few hours. In just a couple of runs, I managed to build a good pile of sticks close to our shelter, then I went back and forth collecting suitable stones and piling them beside the sticks.

'Can't I help with something?' the president asked. 'I feel like a spare part.'

'No, President. You stay where you are.'

He kept offering to help, but I wouldn't let him do anything. He was so useless at being in the wilderness that he made me feel like an expert. For once, I was the best at something, and so I told him to rest while I worked. He sat forward with his forearms on his knees, the pistol beside him, watching my every move.

'You speak good English, Oskari,' he said when I brought the final armful of stones. 'Does everyone in your village speak English?'

'Yes. Some of the older people maybe aren't so good.'

'They teach it at school, I guess.'

'Mm-hm. And we watch American TV.'

'Of course. The power of TV.' He shivered as the wind picked up. 'So, tell me what you're doing with those rocks.'

'This will stop anyone seeing the fire,' I said, building the stones up into a low wall. 'And it will absorb and reflect the heat. Soon it will be nice and warm under here.'

'You really know what you're doing, don't you?' He sounded impressed.

When the wall was almost waist height, I made a small circle of stones on our side of it and took out my fire kit. A little ball of lint and a few scrapes from my fire steel was all I needed to get a flame going, and once that was done, I fed the fire with small sticks until it was strong enough for larger ones.

'Pretty good, Oskari.' The president put out his hands to feel the warmth. 'I can tell you've done that before.'

I sat back and leaned against a rock, putting my arms around my knees. 'One of the things I'm best at. Dad always gets me to build the fire.'

'I wouldn't have any idea how.'

'It's easy really; all you need is a good fire kit. *Every* hunter needs a good fire kit.' I took the plastic tub out of my pocket to show him. 'It has everything I need – fire steel, lint, storm matches – all inside this tight, waterproof tub.'

'Storm matches?'

'For emergencies only,' I said. 'They will light anywhere and they don't go out. You can light them, put them under water, in the soil, wherever you like – and when you take them out, they're still lit.'

'Amazing.' The president shook his head.

'Look.' I unscrewed the lid and took out the tube of storm matches. 'I'll show you.'

'Don't waste them.'

'It's okay.' I took out one of the matches. It was longer than an ordinary match, and almost the entire length of the stem was covered in a red coating. I scraped it against the side of the tube to light it and it flared up right away. I held it up for him to see before sticking it into the soil at my feet. I covered it over, stamped on it, then dug it up. When I took it out, the flame popped into life again.

'Impressive.'

I took my cup of water and put the match into it, dousing the flame. When I removed it from the water, the match flared again so I blew it out, only for it to relight.

'See? With this kit and my knife, I can survive anywhere,' I said, throwing the match on the fire.

'I guess the bow comes in handy, too.'

I glanced at the bow leaning against the rock beside me, and thought about how I had felt when I was standing on the platform in the Place of Skulls, trying to draw it all the way. 'With my knife I could easily make a bow,' I said.

'So why don't you? The one you have is obviously too big.'

'No, it isn't,' I argued. 'It's not too big.'

'Oh. Okay.' The president backed off, sensing that he had touched a nerve.

For a while, neither of us said anything, and I kept feeding the fire until it was just right. When it was ready, I gave the president a thin blanket from my pack so he could take off his clothes and spread them on the rocks by the fire to dry. While he did that, I rummaged through what I had saved from the crashed ATV, asking if he was hungry.

He nodded. 'I guess I am. Haven't had much time to think about it, really, but now that you mention it . . .'

He looked wretched, holding the blanket around him, probably wondering how his whole world had fallen apart. One moment he had been flying in his plane, and the next he was here, sitting on the mountain trying to keep warm. It was still so strange to think that he was Alan William Moore, the President of the United States.

'I have dried reindeer meat,' I said taking a fold of cloth and holding it up.

'Really?' He screwed up his face. 'Reindeer?'

'You don't like it?'

'Never tried it.' His expression said he didn't really want to, either.

I shrugged. 'I have sausages.'

'Now you're talking.'

'Blood sausage it is, then.'

'Wait . . . what did you say?' He leaned closer as if he hadn't heard me properly. '*Blood* sausage?'

'Sure. We make them from pig's blood.'

He detected my hint of a smile and pointed at me. 'You're pulling my leg, aren't you?'

I laughed. 'My dad loves them, but I never liked them much. Don't worry, I have normal sausages.'

The president smiled and shook his finger at me, making me laugh again as I took out a couple of sausages and chose some good sticks to skewer them. I handed one to the president and we held them over the flames until they were black on the outside but heated right through. The smell that came off them was delicious, and my mouth watered as they cooked, then we sat beneath the overhang, close to the warmth of the fire, and settled down to eat.

'They're good,' the president said, waving a hand across his mouth because it was too hot for him.

'The rabbit would have been better.'

'Well, you're doing a great job of looking after me, Oskari, so thank you for that.'

His words made me feel good and I looked over at him, huddled beneath his blanket. 'What is it like to be powerful?'

He almost choked on his food, coughing and spluttering, so I passed him a bottle of water and waited.

The president took a long drink, tipping his head back, then wiped his mouth with a hand and cleared his throat. 'Powerful?' he said with a distant smile. 'That took me by surprise, Oskari. I don't exactly feel powerful sitting here in my shorts.'

'No, but . . . usually you are.'

He became serious. 'Well. I guess I'd say power is . . .

ephemeral. Which means you can't touch it, and it's easy to lose. For example, a few hours ago I could send armies around the globe, and invade foreign soil if I wanted to. Now I can't even order a pizza.' He sighed and took another bite of his sausage.

'I like pizza.'

'Yeah?' He looked up at me. 'Do you have a favourite topping?'

'Pepperoni.'

'Good choice. Tastier than blood sausage, I'd bet. And where do you stand on cookies?'

'Cookies are good.'

'And ice cream?'

'That's good, too.' Mum used to make the best vanilla ice cream. I could almost taste it just thinking about it.

'In that case, when all this is over, I'll invite you to my place. We'll have a blast. Pizza, ice cream and video games. You like video games, right?'

'Right.'

'It's a deal, then.' He finished his sausage and leaned over to take another from me. 'As long as it's okay with your mom and dad, of course.' He skewered the sausage and held it over the flames. 'You never mentioned your mom. Is she a hunter, too?'

I stared at the fire and took a deep breath. 'She died. Last year.'

'Oh . . . I'm sorry . . . I . . .'

'It isn't your fault,' I said, without looking up. 'Why do people always say "sorry" when it isn't their fault?'

He sighed. 'Well, I guess it's because they feel bad

and they wish there was something they could do. And, maybe, because there isn't really anything else to say.'

'Then they should say nothing.'

'Maybe you're right.'

I continued to stare into the flames, watching the way they danced and curled around each other. The heat was fierce on my face. 'She had cancer in her head. She was sick for a long time and then . . .' I gritted my teeth and fought back the tears. My voice was tight in my throat. 'Dad is still very sad. He's not the same as he used to be. I thought that maybe if I got a good trophy it would make him happy, but that's not going to happen now.'

I could feel the president watching me across the fire, leaning back and looking away only when something scuttled across the rocks in the dark. He studied the emptiness beyond the fire for a while, then turned back to me. 'Do you have any brothers or sisters?'

I shook my head and sniffed. 'Mum always said one was more than enough trouble.'

The president laughed gently. 'My mom said something similar whenever I asked her why I didn't have a brother or sister. I guess we have something in common, eh?' He leaned forward to put his food over the fire once more. 'So what made you ask about power?'

'No reason.'

He sat there, waiting for me to go on.

'My father is powerful,' I said. 'In fact, my family is very famous here. Maybe you recognize my dad's name. Tapio. It's the same name as the forest god.'

'I'm sorry. I never heard of him.'

I shrugged. 'You don't know much about hunting.'

'That's true.'

I took the photograph from my pocket and handed it to the president. 'This is my dad.'

He studied it for a while, nodding. 'And that's the bear you told me about.'

'Yes.'

'Wow, that's . . . impressive.'

'In my village, we all do this when we turn thirteen. We come into the forest for a night and a day, and what we kill shows the world what we are as a man.' I remembered Hamara's words, remembered him standing on the platform beside me, doubting that I would manage to hunt anything at all.

'That's what you meant by "trophy" just now?' the president asked.

'Yes.'

He looked up from the photo. 'So what does it mean if you kill a bear?'

'That the man is brave and strong.'

'And now it's your turn, huh?'

'Tomorrow is my birthday. When morning comes, I will be a man. "A boy sets out into the wilderness, but it is a man who will return." That's what Hamara said.'

'Hamara?'

'He's our elder.'

The president watched me for a while longer, still nodding as if he understood something. Now he knew why I was out here alone. 'And I guess I've messed it all up for you. I'm sorry.'

'Mum used to say the buck would be my animal because it means the man will be quick and smart and inde . . . indep . . .' The English word for it was on the tip of my tongue but refused to come out.

'You mean "independent"?'

'Yes.'

'Well, I think you've got those things covered already.' He glanced down at the bow and pointed at it with a tilt of his chin. 'And that?'

'I have to use it. It's the traditional bow; the one we all use. It's at least a hundred years old.'

'Really? It doesn't look that old.'

'It's been well looked after.'

'No one would know if you used a different one,' he said. 'One that wasn't so big.'

'I would know.'

'Of course you would. You're very honest, Oskari, and that's a good thing to be. You're stronger than you think, too.' He handed the photo back to me. 'You look like him.'

'We're made from the same wood, me and my dad.' I tucked the photo away. 'He believes in me even though everyone else thinks I'm a bad hunter. When Hamara gave me the bow, I couldn't even draw it all the way and some of the boys laughed, but I decided I would try my hardest to make Dad proud. Now, though, I'll have to be rescued and we'll both look bad.'

'These are exceptional circumstances, Oskari.'

'Doesn't matter. You have to be tough in Finland.' I took a bite of my sausage. 'Everyone has to see that you are tough.'

'Well, you got us away from those men and brought us here. You covered our tracks, made a fire and shelter. Fed us. I can tell everyone that.' The president leaned forward and turned the skewer in his fingers as he spoke. 'Anyway, instead of being tough, you can just look tough. And let me tell you, I'm a world expert on that.' The firelight reflected from his face and glittered in his eyes as he spoke. 'Hell, I read self-help books and eat cookies. Morris laughs at me because I can't even do ten push-ups.' He looked down when he said that, and I knew he would be thinking about the bodies we had found on the rocks.

'Let me tell you a story,' he said. 'When I gave my last State of the Union address, I suddenly needed to pee just before it was about to begin. So I dashed to the toilet, with only minutes to go, and in my hurry, I tried to . . . ah, "replace" myself a little too quickly, and some of it splashed. Hit my upper trouser zone.'

I burst out laughing. I couldn't help it. The idea of the President of the United States peeing on his own trousers was ridiculous.

'Exactly.' He shrugged. 'Happens to us all, eh? Anyway, moments later, I had to walk out, on to the floor of the House Chamber, which is a huge room filled with important people. The eyes of America were on me, and I had to go out there with a sizable wet patch on my groin.'

'Oh my God.'

'Look it up sometime,' he said, 'and notice the way I'm

holding my notes to obscure the disaster area. And then notice the way I give my address. My voice doesn't shake, my nerve doesn't break, I command the attention of the room. Inside, though, I'm terrified. I'm a mess. I think I'm going to go down in history as the president who peed his pants. But on the outside, I'm a rock.'

'So what happened?'

'No one noticed. The moment passed. And there's only two people on this entire planet that even know it happened. Me, and you.'

'Wow.'

'You won't tell anyone, right?'

'As long as you don't tell anyone I missed the rabbit.'

'Deal.'

Together, we pulled invisible zips over our mouths, locked them and threw the keys into the fire.

The president laughed, good and loud, and I laughed with him, but after that he didn't say much, and I watched him as we finished our meal and licked our fingers clean. From time to time the breeze would catch the fire and it would flare up and buzz, then retreat into the circle of rocks, but that was the only sound.

A little later, as we both sat, lost in our own thoughts, the wind picked up and a light flurry of snow began to tumble in the chilly mountain air.

'Snow?' the president said. 'In spring?'

'We're high up now,' I replied. 'And very far north. It can snow at any time of year.'

'This place really *is* tough.'

I smiled. 'Well, your clothes are probably dry now.

131

You should get dressed.'

'Yeah.' He checked them and said they were good enough, then redressed and sat back down in his place, exactly as he had been before. The small badge on his lapel glinted in the firelight, and I could just about make out the blue and red of the US flag.

The president's expression was serious and he was biting his lower lip as he stared into the flames. He rubbed a hand over his bald head. 'You asked what it's like to be powerful, Oskari. Well, one thing is that you're always wondering who you can trust.'

'You can trust me,' I said.

'I don't mean you. I mean that someone set this up,' he said. 'Someone sabotaged my men's parachutes. I have a feeling it was someone I thought I could trust.'

'Who?'

'The man we saw at the crash site.'

'Hazar?'

He shook his head.

'The man in the suit?'

'I think I know who it is. I don't want to believe it, and I'm not sure how he even managed it but . . . no.' He shook his head again. 'It couldn't be.' He fell into silence once more, and I could tell he wasn't going to say anything else.

'I think maybe you should sleep now.' I stifled a yawn. 'I'll keep watch.'

'I should do that. I'm the adult—' He stopped, as if he realized he was saying something I wouldn't like. 'I *owe* you.'

'You don't owe me anything, President. I was going to come here anyway. I was going to stay up all night and hunt. I will keep watch instead, and if a buck or a bear walks across my path, I will be ready to kill it.' I held up the bow so he could see I had it ready. 'Maybe I can kill a trophy after all.'

'And what if those men come?'

'I'll hear them before they ever see us.'

'Well, make sure you wake me if you hear anything. I'll keep this close.' He showed me the pistol, then lay down in the dirt and placed the weapon on the ground beside him. He hesitated, as if he was going to suggest he keep watch again, but I shook my head at him.

'Go to sleep,' I said.

He sighed, then threw the blanket across himself and moved about until he was comfortable.

'Goodnight, President,' I said.

'Goodnight, Oskari.'

HAPPY BIRTHDAY

The president was a snorer, which was funny at first, but grew annoying after a while. As the night went on, his grunts and snuffles competed with the cold wind that whistled around the plateau, bringing the snow. The fire was warm, though, and we were well protected under the overhang, and despite my efforts to stay awake, my eyes began to close. I shook my head, slapped my face and walked around for a bit. I went out into the cold air beyond the overhang, collecting more wood, but nothing stopped the drowsiness. I was exhausted, and as soon as I sat down, my mind began to cloud over.

Eventually I lost the battle, and sleep smothered me, bringing strange visions. Hamara looking down at me, disapproving, while Dad hung his head in shame. The ATV, crushed by a tree, damaged beyond repair. Fireballs raining from a coal-black sky, and Patu's dead eyes staring at me as I struggled to draw the bow. The images all mixed together in a nightmare that sloshed like heavy water in my head, and through it all, there was that grunting noise.

Myygh! Myygh!

That's what woke me up. A long, loud grunt that startled my eyes open. For a second I didn't know where I was and I stumbled to my feet, gripping the bow that had been across my lap. The morning air was cool and fresh, and there was still a fluttering of snow in the air. The fire had burned right down to embers that could only manage a weak glow in the gathering daylight. Bleary-eyed, I looked about as last night's events came rushing back to grip me like an icy fist. It was as if a hand had punched right through me and grabbed my insides and started to squeeze them tight.

But there was light behind the thick clouds, morning was here, and that meant we only had to last a few more hours before Dad would come looking for us. And the man in the suit had said that the president's soldiers would be looking for us by dawn. Rescue was on its way.

I looked down at the president, lying on his side, and I still couldn't quite believe that the actual President of the USA was right there, huddled under my old blanket. When the noise came again, though – that long, loud grunt – I realized it wasn't coming from him. He was breathing heavily, but not snoring any more, and—

Myygh! Myygh!
An elk! That was the sound of an elk calling!

My brain finally kicked into gear and I dropped into a crouch, looking out across the plateau, squinting through the snow that danced in the wind. The covering that had fallen in the night was powdery and thin, made patchy by the darkness of the rocks that protruded from beneath it. Each breath of fresh mountain air stung my nostrils, and every time I exhaled, it rose in wisps around my face. I stayed that way, scanning the terrain, but there was nothing to see other than scruffy grass poking through the snow, and a few straggly trees with spindly branches. There was an elk out there somewhere, though, so I crept away from the overhang, nocking an arrow into the bowstring, and kept low as I moved into the open.

My heart was pounding, and everything about the president was forgotten. Nothing mattered any more. There was an elk close by and I was going to hunt and kill it. It wouldn't escape me like the deer that had run away from the helicopter. This was my trophy, and in spite of everything that had happened, I would carry its head over my back when I left the forest.

Moving slowly and quietly, I made my way across the plateau, scanning the snow for the dung or split-hoof print of an elk.

Myygh! Myygh!
Behind and to my left.

I turned to the place where the plateau gently sloped up and around towards Dad's secret hunting ground, and I remained still, letting my eyes unfocus. My breathing softened and my mind became calm as I waited for my vision to find it. And then, there it was – standing about ten metres higher than my position, at the top of a gentle, rocky incline, dotted with boulders and a couple of scrawny spruce trees.

The elk was huge, with powerful back legs and a gentle hump along the ridge of its back. Its head dipped towards the ground as it foraged for food, and its antlers branched out into a series of deadly points.

I studied the way the snow fell, seeing the fine particles drift downhill. Perfect. I was under the wind. If I remained quiet, I would be able to get close enough to take a shot. The bow was too big, but I was determined to find the strength this time. I must not fail.

As I watched, the elk raised its head and grunted, long and loud.

Myygh! Myygh!

'What the hell was that?'

The words took me by surprise and I snapped around to see the president standing by the firebreak, with the blanket wrapped around his shoulders.

'Happy birthday,' he said, and was about to speak again when he saw the furious expression on my face. I didn't waste any time watching him. I threw him a warning glance, then turned back to the elk.

It had heard the president, and turned its bulky head to look in our direction. It stood perfectly still, muscles tensed.

I did the same. I held my breath, and only one thought raced through my head, over and over again.

Please stay there. Please stay there. Please stay there.

The elk stared at me and I stared back.

Time stood still.

The elk lifted its head a little higher and its nose moved as it tested the wind, searching for a scent. After a moment, it tipped its head right back, so its antlers were almost touching its back, and it opened its mouth once more.

Myygh! Myygh!

Then it trotted away, over the ridge, and disappeared from view.

'No!' I whispered, heart sinking.

I looked back at the president, letting him see how angry I was.

He mouthed the word 'sorry', but I didn't waste any more time. I wouldn't lose it, not this time. Trying to swallow my anger and remain calm, I set off up the slope, following the prints left in the snow, but they were disappearing quickly beneath the fresh fall. With a bit of luck, the animal wouldn't go too far and I would be able to track and catch up with it.

Feeling the wind in my face, I crept up the slope, keeping the bow ready to fire. I took short steps, keeping silent as I moved, being careful not to disturb the small rocks and send them rattling down the slope.

When I reached the top of the incline, I crouched and brought the bow up. I was as excited and nervous as I had ever been. My blood was swooshing in my ears and my cold hands were shaking. I stayed low and concentrated on calming my breathing. I closed my eyes and tried to relax.

A steady heart means a steady hand.

When I began to feel calmer, I swallowed to wet my throat, then opened my mouth and let out the best elk call I had ever done. It was easily as good as Dad's. Better than Hamara's, probably. If the elk were close enough, he would be fooled into staying where he was, casting a curious look in my direction. He would be there when I came over the lip of the slope, and I would have to shoot. I couldn't hesitate. I couldn't afford to miss the chance again.

I called once more, began to draw the bowstring, then stood and moved up on to the level ground.

Beyond the ridge, I was surprised to see a flat meadow surrounded by boulders and pines that swayed in the wind. I had never been to this part of Mount Akka and would not have expected to see something like this so high up. The land was soft and it looked like there was a good covering of grass beneath the snow. It was a perfect place for animals to come and graze. This was Dad's secret hunting ground. I scanned left and right, letting my eyes unfocus, but I felt my heart sink: Once again, I had missed my chance. There was no sign of the elk. It had gone, and its tracks had already disappeared beneath the snow.

Instead, there was something else in the middle of the hunting ground – something that was completely out of place.

It was right there, out in the open.

A large white box.

Everything about this Trial had gone wrong.

All my strength left me and I sagged against the freezer chest, tears stinging my eyes. My shoulders dropped and I hung my head with the shame of knowing that I was a failure. I felt awful. Much worse than I had ever felt in my whole life. I had tried to tell myself that Dad believed in me, that he knew I would bring something good from the forest. But now all that was gone. *Nobody* believed in me. The only reason why Dad had been so sure about sending me out to do the Trial was because he had cheated for me.

'Oskari?'

I wiped my face and looked over at the president. He was standing just at the edge of Dad's fake hunting ground, snow swirling about him.

'Oskari? Are you okay?'

'Go away.' I turned my back on him and wandered towards the trees and rocks on the opposite side of the hunting ground. I rubbed my eyes and sat on a smooth, cold rock, staring down at the wilderness, hating the tears that ran down my cheeks.

The president came after me, his footsteps noisy, his breathing heavy from the exertion of climbing the slope. He sat beside me and leaned back. 'What's wrong?' he asked.

Without saying anything, I passed him the note. The president looked at it and handed it back.

'Did you see the head?' I asked.

'I saw.'

'It's from my dad. He killed that buck so my failure

144

wouldn't humiliate him.' I crumpled the note and threw it down on to the snow. 'Not even my dad believes in me. I'm not a hunter. I'm a nobody.'

'He was probably just trying to help.'

'He thinks I'm a failure.'

'I'm sure that's not true.'

'What, then? Why else would he do this?'

'Because he loves you and wants to help you. You're his son, Oskari.'

I continued to stare at the wilderness below. 'He said I was smart. Is this what he means? Does he think this is smart?'

'Look at me.'

I sighed and turned to look at him, seeing him properly for the first time in daylight. He had a kind face and there was something in his eyes that made me feel even sadder. I didn't want him to feel sorry for me.

'You're not a nobody,' he said. 'You rescued me.'

'Anyone else could have done it.'

'But *you* did it, Oskari. You found me and you helped me. You got me away from those people and you covered our tracks. Who could have done that but a hunter? You kept me safe.'

I shrugged and wiped my nose.

'I believe in you,' he said. 'Here.' He reached up and removed the pin badge from his lapel, then leaned over and attached it to the collar of my jacket. 'Happy birthday. Today you become a man.'

I looked down at the badge, shaped like an American flag, and sniffed. 'I don't feel like one.'

'Well, you—'

A loud bang made us both turn around to see a long streak of white smoke shooting into the sky from somewhere not far behind us. When it reached its peak, the flare exploded like a firework, spreading a glow of red light in all directions as it began to drift back towards the earth.

'Is that what I think it is?' The president didn't take his eyes off it.

'Yes.' My stomach cramped and my scalp tingled. 'They've found us.'

DESTINY APPROACHING

I knew that danger was close, but I had to know *how* close, so I jumped from the rock and ran over to the top of the incline, throwing myself down on my stomach when I reached it. I crawled closer, peering over the top to see Hazar's men by our shelter. Some were standing guard, while others were picking through my belongings.

The suited man we had seen last night waited in the centre of the plateau, and I could see him clearly now; he was about the same age as Dad, but taller and with close-cropped hair. He was good-looking and strong, with broad shoulders and a wide back. He held out something that looked like a mobile phone, and scanned the plateau before typing something into it and looking around again.

'The fire is still warm,' one of Hazar's men called out. 'And their gear is still here, but there are no footprints.'

'The snow's getting heavier. They were here not long ago,' the suited man said. 'The information is good.'

'Morris,' the president said as he crawled alongside me. 'He was on the plane with me. He's the one who put me in the escape pod. He must have sabotaged the other parachutes and jumped out after me.'

'Your bodyguard?' I whispered in disbelief.

'A damn *traitor*,' the president replied through gritted teeth. 'I didn't want to believe it.'

'But how did he find us?' I watched Morris, wondering who I was most afraid of: him or Hazar.

'Someone is helping him. Someone is sending him information on that handset. It's the only explanation.'

'But how would anyone else know where we are?' I had done everything I could to cover our tracks.

'There'll be satellites trained on this forest, Oskari, all of them looking for me.'

'Like in a video game?'

'Yeah, maybe, and someone who is watching the satellite could be telling Morris what they're seeing. Damn it. I can't believe it . . . that man took a bullet for me.'

From the distance, the faint *thucka-thucka-thucka* of a helicopter grew, and a small black dot appeared in the white sky over the trees far below.

'We have to go, President.' I started shuffling backwards. 'Come on.'

When we were out of sight, we stood and ran across the snow and rocks, past the freezer towards the trees. As we came close to them, though, the president stopped.

'What are you doing?' I hissed, trying to keep my voice low. 'We need to hurry!'

The president shook his head and reached into his pocket, removing the pistol he had taken from Otis. 'We need to go our separate ways.'

'What?' I grabbed his arm, trying to make him follow me. 'Come on. They'll be here any moment.'

'It doesn't make a damn bit of difference, don't you see? Look at the tracks we're leaving – you know better than I do how bad that is. And if I'm right about the satellites up there looking at us, they'll see every move we make. We could wave to the people watching.'

I looked up at the sky, snowflakes falling on my face. 'For real?'

'Yes, for real. And if Morris is getting information about where we are, then it doesn't matter what we do. In daylight, they'll see us wherever we go.'

'But they can't see through trees, right?'

'I guess.'

'So let's go into the trees. There's less snow in there, too; we won't leave tracks. Further down the mountain there won't be *any*. We'll stay in the forest and—'

'No.' The president pulled his arm away. '*You* go, Oskari. Use all your knowledge of these mountains and forests to get as far away from here as you can, as fast as you can.'

Still the helicopter approached, the black speck growing as it came closer, the sound of its pounding engine becoming louder.

'Go, Oskari, you've done enough. I can't put you in any more danger.'

'But what about you?' I was starting to panic. Any moment now and the men would come up the rise to find us standing here.

'I can look after myself.'

'No, President, I don't think you can.' Feeling the urgency building to bursting point, I grabbed for his arm again. 'But what if—'

He pulled away. 'If whoever is helping Morris can see me, then so can my people. They will be here soon; it's only a matter of time.' He put his hand on my shoulder and looked me right in the eye. 'Oskari, I need you to believe in me – like I believe in you.'

I wondered if there was anything I could do to make him change his mind. The truth was that I liked him and I didn't want him to put himself in danger.

Before I could say anything, though, the president spat in his hand and offered it to me, saying, 'Thank you for being my friend, Oskari.'

I considered his gesture as a thousand thoughts rushed through my head. Maybe he was right. Maybe I should save myself and leave him to face Hazar alone. After all, this wasn't my fight. And, anyway, the president's Navy SEALs would be here any moment.

Almost without realizing I was doing it, I spat in my own hand and we shook.

'It's time for you to go,' the president said.

Still I hesitated.

'Now, Oskari! Go!'

The way he spoke startled me, and I looked up at him as he pushed me away.

'Go!'

So I turned and ran, sprinting across the hunting ground as if the devil was grabbing at my heels. I scurried up the boulders at the far edge and jumped down into the forest, disappearing into the trees and leaving my new friend behind me.

Everything was a blur. Thoughts boiled in my mind. The deer head. The note. Hazar. Morris. They all swirled about as I ran and ran and ran. My arms and legs moved without me even thinking about it. My whole body burned with the adrenaline that was raging around my blood, fuelling my muscles to move harder and faster.

I ducked branches and skirted around trees and boulders without a clear idea of where I was going or what I was going to do. My boots pounded the forest floor like a drumbeat that would never stop.

Except, they did stop.

When an image of the president appeared in my head like a photograph, blocking out everything else, it was as if I had run into a wall of solid rock.

I came to a sudden halt and stood there, chest heaving for breath, with that picture still in my head.

It was an image of the president, my new friend,

wrapped in a blanket, cold and tired and afraid, and I knew I was the only person who could help him. He had said that there would be people on their way to save him, but they would be too late. The president needed me to do something for him *now*. He needed help *now*.

I touched the pin badge on the collar of my jacket and remembered what my new friend had said to me: *I believe in you*. Well, what use was that if all I could do was run away and abandon him? There was no other hope for him – I had to do something. I should never have left him.

Realizing what I was about to do, I turned and looked back, feeling afraid and excited and angry all at once. I was terrified of the men with guns, especially Morris and Hazar, but they were in *my* place and they had no right to be here. This was *my* wilderness. *My* mountain. And today *I* was the king here. Satellites and helicopters and guns wouldn't be of any use to them if we could disappear into the forest.

'I'm coming,' I said as I started to jog back. 'I'm coming to help you, President.'

Everything was different now that I wasn't running away in fear. I had decided to be the hunter rather than the hunted, and my senses understood that. My mind became calmer and I was aware of everything around me. I heard every rustle of partridge in the undergrowth, every call of every bird. I felt the breeze on my face and the ground beneath my feet.

When I reached the boulders skirting the hunting ground, the snow had stopped and the sky was beginning to clear. I pressed myself against the cold grey rock and listened.

In the distance, the thumping of the helicopter approached.

Thucka-thucka-thucka.

I eased around the rock, slipping between two large, smooth boulders and boosting myself up on a smaller one so I could look over without being seen. My view of the hunting ground was excellent – the surrounding rocks and trees, and the freezer chest right in the middle.

The president was nowhere to be seen, and for one terrifying moment, I thought they had found him already, but as I scanned the area, Hazar's men appeared over the lip of the slope that led down to our camp. Four of them, moving in a line through the snow, automatic weapons held high. They spread out as they came on to the hunting ground, sweeping their sub-machine guns in arcs, moving slowly.

The president appeared from behind a boulder a metre or so to my right. He stepped out with his arms raised, the pistol straight out in front of him. Hazar's men noticed him almost immediately and swung their weapons around to point at him, but the president wasn't going to be taken without a fight.

He was the first to pull the trigger.

There was no loud bang, though. No crackle of gunfire or falling bodies.

Instead, there was a faint click and a moment of nothing.

The men stared at the president, and he stared back

for a fraction of a second. Then he was turning the pistol in his hand, looking at it as if it had betrayed him, and—

Morris appeared from the rocks behind the president.

The bodyguard moved quickly, crossing the distance to the president in a split second. He slipped his left arm around my friend's neck, while his other hand went straight for the pistol, grasping it hard and twisting it out of the president's grip. Before he had a chance to react, the president was disarmed and Morris was pressing the barrel of the weapon into the soft skin under his chin.

'Next time you want to shoot someone,' Morris said, 'take off the safety catch.'

He took the gun away from the president's chin, and in one quick movement released the clip so that it slid out on to the ground, then threw the weapon to one side and pushed the president into the hunting ground.

My friend stumbled forwards, falling to his hands and knees, but he was quick to get back to his feet and turn around to face his bodyguard.

'Why?' he asked. 'Why are you doing this?'

Morris shook his head. 'You're too damn stupid to work it out, aren't you?'

'I thought you were a friend.'

'You don't have friends,' Morris said. 'You're the President of the United States. You *can't* have friends.'

'But you put your life on the line for me. What's changed?'

'This.' Morris tapped his chest. 'The bullet I took for you. Your legacy right here, working its way into my heart. I have a family, too, remember. They'll need money when I'm gone – and it's only a matter of time.'

'You could've retired. You had the option. I—'

'Money. And I'm not talking about some pitiful pension, I'm talking about the kind of money that comes from handing a man like you over to a man like that.' He raised a finger and pointed at the sky. 'That's your destiny approaching.'

'This is about *money*?' Betrayal and disappointment were clear in the president's voice.

'Isn't it always?'

The president shook his head. 'And I thought we were friends.'

'You thought wrong.'

The helicopter was growing louder by the second; it would be here any moment. I looked left and right, trying to think what I could do, but with all those armed men in the hunting ground, I was helpless and useless. There was nothing I could do to help my friend. Nothing at all.

'By the way,' Morris said, stepping towards the president. 'Where's your little helper? Abandoned you, eh?'

'I don't know what you're talking about.'

Morris stood toe to toe with the president and looked him in the eye. 'Sure you do. The kid who popped you out of the rescue pod. Drove that ATV we found. Lit a fire for you last night and gave you a blanket.'

'I don't know, Morris. I guess if you're too damn stupid to work it out—'

Morris struck out with his right hand, hard and fast, smashing the president in the kidneys. He cried out in pain and dropped to his knees, but Morris didn't leave it at that. He put up both fists and began to rain blows on the president, hitting him over and over again as the helicopter finally came in to land.

WHAT THE FOREST WANTED

The thundering engine was deafening as the black helicopter came to a hover over the hunting ground and began descending towards the snow, creating a storm of its own. The skids on its underside touched down, then rose about a metre as the pilot corrected the angle before settling on to the ground. The awful beat of the engine died and the smell of aviation fuel carried on the wind. The rotor blades slowed and became still, creaking a little as they settled.

Immediately there was a clinking of kit and crunching of boots as the soldiers hurried across to the helicopter, ducking as they went even though the rotor blades had stopped spinning.

Morris stayed where he was, reaching down to grab the president by the scruff of his jacket and drag him to his knees.

'You're about to meet someone who's been looking for you, *Bill*.' He spoke the president's name with sarcasm and disrespect. 'His name is Hazar and he's the illegitimate son of one of the richest oil sheiks in the Gulf. You know what? I have a feeling you're not going to like him very much.'

'He won't get anything from me.' The president sounded strong, but I knew he was trying to look tough. Underneath it all, he was tired and afraid. There was disappointment, too, at having been betrayed by the man he thought was his friend. I imagined it would be ten times worse than the disappointment I had felt when I had found Dad's note.

Morris laughed. 'Oh, Hazar doesn't want anything from you. This isn't about politics or ideology. It's not even about religion, *Bill*, he's just a certified Grade A psychopath who thinks of himself as a hunter. Which means you're in a lot of trouble. You see, all he wants to do is kill you.'

The president didn't say or do anything. He just knelt in the snow with his head hanging so that his chin was almost on his chest. His breath billowed around him in clouds. He was exhausted and beaten, probably knowing that no one was coming to help him now. He had been captured and would have to suffer whatever came next.

I looked about the hunting ground, trying to think of something, *any*thing I could do to help, but we were in the middle of nowhere and all I had was my bow and my knife. Maybe if I could make some kind of distraction . . .

The sound of the helicopter door sliding open made me look around to see Hazar step down on to the snow. He put his hands in the small of his back and stretched, turning his neck from side to side as if it had been an uncomfortable journey. I could almost hear the creak of his tight-fitting leather jacket as he moved, and I gritted my teeth, imagining myself firing an arrow straight into his heart. Right then, I hated that man more than I had ever hated anything. All the anger I had for everything else was directed at him. Only him.

Hazar looked around at his men, nodding with satisfaction. Then, without turning back to the helicopter, he reached up with his right hand.

'My rifle.'

Without a second's delay, one of the soldiers passed Hazar's weapon from inside, putting it right into his hand. Hazar sniffed, hefted the weapon, then sauntered across the hunting ground towards the president.

Behind him, one of his men jumped down from the helicopter carrying a tripod with a large camera fastened to the top. He jogged to catch up with Hazar, then followed a couple of paces behind.

As he passed the freezer chest and the deer head, Hazar glanced down for a second, but didn't stop. He didn't even stop in front of the president, but walked around behind him and ordered Morris to move aside.

The man with the camera stopped a couple of metres away from where the president was kneeling, and set the tripod on the ground.

'You know the tradition,' Hazar said, 'in which the hunter poses for a photograph with his prey?'

The president remained silent.

'Well, it's good to observe the old ways of doing things, don't you think, Mr President?' Hazar put his boot on the president's back and kicked him forwards into the snow. 'Lie down.'

The president tried to turn and look at the hunter, but Hazar kicked him hard in the kidneys. 'Lie down,' he spat.

I couldn't bear to see my friend like that, beaten and defenceless. He was coughing and groaning, writhing in pain on the ground.

Hazar put one boot on him and held his rifle in both hands. He put his shoulders back and stuck out his chest. The camera clicked several times and the cameraman nodded at Hazar.

'You got a good one?' Hazar asked.

'Yes, sir.'

In that instant, I saw the board in the Hunting Lodge with all those photographs pinned to it. I saw the one of Dad with the bear on his back, but mostly I saw the ones of the other men, standing with the bow in their hands and their trophy at their feet. Is that really what all this was about? It was a hunt?

And that's when it came to me. Like a bolt out of the sky that dusted away the clouds and showed me the real reason why that plane had crashed across *my* path and knocked *me* from the ATV. The real reason why *I* had seen the red light blinking in the sky and found the pod. The real reason why *I* had found the president.

Because this was what the forest wanted.

My wilderness. My president.

Hamara's words echoed in my head. *The forest is a harsh judge. It gives each of us what we deserve. We must know how to listen and fight tooth and nail for our prey.*

Now I understood. I was supposed to rescue him. *This* was my Trial. I had not come into the forest to kill something – I had come here to *save* something.

All I had to do was figure out how.

TROPHY

'Okay, you've had your fun,' Morris said. 'Now let's get this over with. Finish him off.'

Hazar threw Morris an irritated look, then took a deep breath and stepped back a few paces. He raised his rifle, tucking it against his shoulder, and aimed it at the back of the president's head.

I couldn't bear to look. I didn't want to see them kill him. But I stopped myself from closing my eyes or looking away, because I knew I had to do something. It was now or never. A few more seconds and Hazar would pull the trigger and the president would be as dead as Patu.

No.

I took a deep breath, ready to shout at the top of my lungs.

No.

I didn't have much of a plan other than to distract them, maybe make them chase me into the forest. If they thought there was a witness, maybe they wouldn't kill the president. Maybe they would wait until they had caught me first – which they wouldn't. I would be too fast and too clever for them. One word was all I had to shout.

No.

When I opened my mouth, though, the word already forming, someone else said it for me.

'No.' Hazar lowered his rifle and shook his head. 'Not like this.'

'What?' Morris looked at him in disbelief. 'Just get on with it. Let's do this and leave.'

'I have a better idea.'

'A better idea? What the hell are you talking about?'

'I don't want him dead. Not yet. I want him *fresh*.'

'Fresh?' Morris was confused. 'What the hell does that mean?'

Hazar put his rifle over his shoulder and took his phone from his pocket. 'Thank goodness for satellite phones.' He used his thumbs to type a message as he spoke. 'This one will work anywhere on earth; just like yours. I contacted my taxidermist about some of the logistics of dealing with a human cadaver.'

'What?' Morris looked like he couldn't believe his ears.

'Well, apparently if I'm going to stuff him and mount him, it's best that the body is as fresh as possible.' Hazar continued to type, eyes fixed on the small screen.

'My God, you're going to *stuff* him?'

'What else should one do with a hunting trophy?'

'You're insane.'

'And you, my friend, are a very rich man.' Hazar put his phone back into his pocket and looked up at Morris. 'I have just transferred ten million dollars into the agreed bank account. It was a good hunt, thank you.' He turned to the man with the camera. 'That freezer chest is a gift I can't ignore. Let's get the president inside, and then we'll be on our way.'

The man nodded, folded the tripod, and hurried back to the helicopter. He stored it inside and returned with two other men, going straight to the president. They hauled him to his feet and marched him over to Dad's freezer chest.

'What? No!' The president struggled against them.

'Damn it.' Morris was growing more and more angry. 'Why don't you just bring him in the helicopter with us?'

'There's not enough room,' Hazar said. 'This will have to do.'

'I already shot one of your men. There's enough room.'

'A place which you will now occupy.' Hazar raised his weapon to point at Morris. 'Unless you want to give it up for the president?'

Morris gritted his teeth and glared at Hazar. 'Just get a move on. It won't be long before this place is crawling with Navy SEALs.' He took his phone from his pocket and held it up to Hazar, the screen glowing. 'Everything we can see, they can see. Look!'

'I don't care about that,' Hazar said, glancing over at his men. They had removed the buck's head and were struggling to lift the president into the freezer chest.

'Well, you should, because the longer we stay here, the less chance we have of getting away.'

'Please,' the president managed to call. He looked over at Hazar. 'Please don't . . .'

'Oh, my apologies, Mr President,' Hazar shouted back. 'First class is full.' He smiled at his own joke as his men forced the president down.

I stared in disbelief as my friend disappeared from view, but as he did, he looked across the hunting ground, right past Hazar and Morris, and I was sure he saw me. I don't know how, I was so well hidden, but our eyes seemed to meet and hold for a few seconds. We were locked together like that, linked because it was what the wilderness wanted. I understood now that our lives were bound together like the threads of a rope, and that I would not lose him. He was mine; I just had to fight for him.

Then he was gone, pushed right down into the chest, and the men closed the lid on him. They locked the latch, wrapped green cargo straps around the white box and fastened them together to keep the lid shut.

Hazar watched as the men spooled a thick wire from the underside of the helicopter and ran it through the cargo straps holding the freezer chest shut, then he smiled at Morris and said, 'See. That didn't take long.'

'With that weight underneath, it'll slow us down,' Morris replied.

'Relax; we just bagged the biggest prize on the planet. Try to enjoy it.' Hazar raised a hand and made a circling motion before heading back to the helicopter.

'I would have enjoyed it more if you'd just killed him,' Morris grumbled.

As the men climbed aboard, the engine started and the rotors began to turn.

TOOTH AND NAIL

The forest is a harsh judge.

Hamara's words repeated in my head as I slipped down from the boulder and secured the bow across my back. The quiver was tight with moss and the arrows were snug.

It gives each of us what we deserve.

There was no need to move quietly. With the helicopter blades churning the air, lifting the snow into a flurry, no one was going to hear me, so I sprinted along the edge of the hunting ground, keeping out of sight. Dodging through a collection of gaunt silver birch, and leaping over rocks, I skirted around so I was behind the helicopter.

We must know how to listen . . .

I stopped behind two narrow pines that grew together like twins, and pressed myself close to them. Drawing my knife, I watched the last man climb aboard.

. . . and fight tooth and nail for our prey.

As soon as he was in, I began to run. My boots were light on the ground despite the whirlwind. Snow and soil and pine needles spun in the air, but I ignored the stinging clouds of grit that battered my face. I gripped my knife tight in my fist and ran, ran, ran.

My eyes were fixed on the freezer. That was my target. I had to get to it before the helicopter took off.

The forest is a harsh judge.

My arms were like pistons; my legs were steel cords.

It gives each of us what we deserve.

I gritted my teeth and summoned all my strength as the helicopter door slid shut.

We must know how to listen . . .

The freezer was just a few metres away. I was almost there. Not far.

. . . and fight tooth and nail for our prey.

A couple of paces from the freezer, I launched myself at it, arms outstretched.

I hit it with a solid thud and scrambled on top. My camouflage netting rippled around me and the draught ripped the hat from my head as I slipped the blade of my knife under the first of the green nylon cargo straps. One look at the metal rope securing the box to the underside of the helicopter had told me I had no hope of cutting it, but maybe the cargo straps would be easier. The knife was sharp, but the nylon was tough and I sawed the steel backwards and forwards, slicing through the material bit by bit.

The helicopter skids lifted off the ground and began to rise higher and higher, taking the steel rope up into the air. As the metal cord tightened, I knew I didn't have much time. There were three cargo straps to cut through, and only a few more seconds to manage it. My head buzzed with fear and excitement, but the first doubt was beginning to snake in. When I had been running, I hadn't thought for a second that I wouldn't succeed, but now it looked *certain* that I wouldn't.

The first cargo strap gave way to my knife, splitting apart and flying away in the draught created by the rotors. Immediately, I went to the next one, slipping the blade underneath it, and—

The steel cord tightened against the freezer, making it lurch, and in less than a heartbeat it was off the ground, rising into the air with me still on top of it.

My left hand was gripping the cargo strap so tight that my knuckles had gone white. I stared at it and told my fingers to open. I willed my hand to let go, so that I could drop safely to the earth, but it refused. Fear and determination kept it tight around the cargo strap and nothing I could do would make it open. It was as if my body had decided to stay with the president – to fight tooth and nail for my prey.

Within seconds it was too late anyway. The helicopter was rising quickly.

Without even realizing it I slipped my other hand, still holding the knife, under the cargo strap as far as my elbow. I hooked my whole arm around the strong nylon and hung on for dear life as we rose higher and higher over the forest.

The day Dad first made me jump off the waterfall into Lake Tuonela, I thought I was going to drown. I thought a *näkki* was going to drag me down to a grim, watery death. I had been terrified. But the fear I had felt that day was nothing compared to what I felt as I hung on to that chest, swinging in the wind as it trailed behind the helicopter. I was frozen by fear, the way a rabbit can be frozen in fear at night if you point a powerful torch at it.

I couldn't move a muscle. Everything was locked tight. My arms were like stone, clinging on to the cargo straps, and my legs were like a vice, grasping the freezer as if they might crush it. My eyes were squeezed shut so tightly that they hurt.

The wind raced around me, rushing under my jacket, flapping my camouflage, buffeting the freezer chest. Everything seemed to be vibrating and humming and it battered my ears so I couldn't hear anything except for the roaring rush of it swirling around my head.

For what felt like a very long time, I stayed that way, swinging wildly beneath the helicopter with my eyes shut and nothing going through my head other than fear. But fear like that can't last for ever, and it eventually began to dull. It was still there – I was still afraid – just not as much. Being scared was not going to save my life and it wasn't going to save the president's, and as my brain finally started to work properly again, I opened my eyes.

Right away, tears welled up in response to the wind, and they streaked back along my cheeks just like when I had ridden the ATV fast through the forest. I blinked to clear my blurry vision, then took a deep breath of cold, fresh air and forced myself to look around.

The sight of the wilderness below me was awesome. Amazing. Terrifying.

It was the most incredible thing I had ever seen in my life. The treetops sped past beneath me as we headed down the slopes of Mount Akka towards the forested wilderness, a sea that exploded with light and dark green. There was no snow here, though, just a thin mist that hung over the ground among the trees, as if a huge ghost had risen up from the dark soil and spread itself through the forest, obscuring the bracken. Hardly able to take my eyes off it, I looked about, seeing the crags of distant mountains breaking up from the forest and pushing their way into the sky. I saw clouds tinted orange by the sun, and mountain streams glittering like rivers of diamonds.

When I looked up, though, I saw Morris leaning out from the side of the helicopter, looking right at me.

The speed at which we were travelling and the movement of the freezer chest made his face unclear and monstrous. I couldn't quite make out his features, but he was a picture of fury. His eyes were wide, dark holes, and his mouth was tight and grim as he pointed a submachine gun at me, ready to fire.

A quick rattle and the weapon kicked back at his shoulder, making him shudder. The sound of the wind and the helicopter drowned the shots so they were little more than faint pops, and the swinging of the freezer disrupted his aim, sending his bullets wide. He tried to correct himself, moving the weapon in time with the freezer, ready to fire again, but a pair of gloved hands reached out from inside the helicopter and grabbed him.

It had to be Hazar. I would have recognized those leather gloves anywhere.

Morris looked to his right, shouting something at Hazar, and he tried to pull away. There was a brief struggle before Morris lost his grip on the weapon and it tumbled away, swallowed by the mist that hung in the wilderness below.

Morris grimaced at me, then disappeared into the helicopter, only to be replaced by Hazar, who looked down with a big grin and pointed at me before pointing at the forest below. He waggled his fingers as if he was waving at me and then retreated from view.

As soon as he was gone, the helicopter banked to one side and changed direction. The freezer chest swung out to the opposite direction, moving in a wide arc. I clung on as hard as I could when it changed a second time, banking the other way. The steel rope holding the freezer went slack for a fraction of a second, then snapped taut again, almost throwing me off. My left hand came free of the cargo straps and I slipped to one side, losing the grip I'd had with my legs. Pitching across the freezer, I slid off the side and was left hanging by one arm. The knife, still gripped tightly in my hand, caught me across one cheek with a shallow stinging cut.

They were trying to throw me off. They were going to kill me.

I pulled hard, swinging around to grab hold with my left hand. I managed to grasp the cargo straps and, with a huge effort, dragged myself back on to the freezer – but only just in time for the helicopter to change direction again and drop lower in the sky. This time I swung out to the other side, and even though I was better prepared and managed to stay on, I knew it was only a matter of time before they succeeded.

When the helicopter stabilized, I looked up to see Hazar lean out and glance down at me. He didn't grin this time; he grimaced and disappeared once more, and the helicopter banked again, making the freezer lurch beneath me.

Once more, my face came close to my knife, but there was nothing I could do. I couldn't release my hold on the straps and I couldn't let the knife go. It was one of my most important possessions. It was also my only means of releasing the freezer chest from the helicopter – something I now realized was not impossible, because in their attempts to shake me off, the helicopter was descending.

The treetops loomed closer and closer and I knew this was my best chance. I couldn't see the ground, covered in mist as it was, but I was sure that if I could cut through the straps now, it wouldn't be so far to fall. I could save both the president and myself.

My muscles were aching and my hands were burning, but I tightened my thighs around the freezer and secured my left arm, using my right to slide the knife under one of the two remaining straps. I pulled upwards with as much pressure as I could manage, and began sawing at the nylon.

The freezer struck the first treetop with a terrible shudder. It jolted hard and twisted to one side, starting to spin, and I looked up, seeing the world rushing around and around me. My stomach heaved as a feeling of dizzy sickness welled up, but I shook my head and went back to cutting, holding tight with my left hand.

Still the helicopter flew lower, dropping me deeper among the trees, where the mist swirled about in whirlpools, churned by the rotors. Branches slammed against the freezer, bending and snapping. The noise was incredible, as if I was in the centre of a hurricane, but I kept on with my task. There was nothing else for me to do. There was nothing else I *could* do. Hazar was determined to shake me off, but I was not going to abandon my friend. Not when we were so close.

I looked up through the mist and branches and saw a spot in the near distance that would be perfect. There was a rise in the land, a place where no trees grew and the ground was brown with mud. If I could cut the straps as we reached it, there wouldn't be far for us to fall. Just a few metres into the dirt. If we were lucky, there would be no rocks and we'd have a soft landing.

The nylon strap gave way with a sudden release of tension and I wasted no time in starting on the next one.

Not far now.

I slipped the steel of my blade beneath it and began cutting as the branches whipped against me, stinging and scraping. My eyes were streaming and there was blood on my hands and face, but it was as if I had been possessed by some kind of demon. I was no longer scared; I was angry.

'I'm not going to die!' I screamed at the top of my voice. 'I'm not going to die! I'm not going to—'

The freezer slammed into a thick tree trunk with a sickening crunch and my legs lost their grip. I jerked forwards, back-flipping over the top of the freezer so I buckled against the trunk for a fraction of a second before the helicopter dragged the chest onwards, sending it spinning through the trees. My left arm was tight under the cargo strap, and my shoulder felt as if it had been wrenched out of its socket, but I was still secure. My body swung out to one side, though, and when I twisted and reached up to haul myself back on to the freezer, I lost my grip on my knife. It slid across the top of the chest, spinning like a propeller, skittered over the side, and was gone.

Lying face down on top of the freezer, I knew that all hope was lost now. Without my knife, I would never be able to cut the president free. How could I fight tooth and nail if I didn't even have my most important weapon? All I could do was wait for the rise in the land beneath and let myself drop; try to save myself.

'I'm sorry, President,' I said, pressing my bloody cheek against the top of the freezer. 'I have to go.'

I looked up at the helicopter one last time to see Hazar staring down at me with an ugly smile on his face. He waved again, waggling his fingers, and I turned away from him, something catching my eye. A quick flash of light drawing my attention. My knife. It was right there, wedged against the side of the freezer chest, caught under the last of the cargo straps.

I could still do this!

We were almost at the muddy ground, but there was still time.

I wriggled forwards and reached over the side of the freezer, touching my fingertips to the handle of the knife.

Just a little further.

Stretching as far as I could, I wrapped my fingers around the hilt, and twisted it so the blade was against the nylon. I pushed hard and drew it towards me, feeling it bite into the edge of the strap, making the first cut. Straight away, I forced the knife down again, and frayed edges sprang up as the sharp steel sliced through a section of the nylon.

The freezer smashed into another tree, spinning to the left and swinging out to crash through some smaller branches, but I hung on tight with my left hand and turned the knife so the point was wedged against the hard plastic casing of the freezer. I tried to ignore the sickly feeling of spinning and the battering of the branches clawing at me, and I drew the knife up for the last time.

There was a sense of release. A moment of hanging in the air.

Then we were falling into the mist.

WHAT WE DESERVE

The drop was so quick and so sudden, it felt as if I had left my insides somewhere up in the sky. An overwhelming light-headedness washed over me and I didn't even think about what was going to happen when we hit the ground. All I could think was that I had succeeded. I had won. The freezer chest was free and I had managed to get the president away from Hazar and Morris.

We descended like a landing plane, travelling down and forwards at the same time, carried by the momentum of the helicopter that had been dragging us. Except we weren't heading for a flat landing strip, we were heading for a muddy bank at the edge of the trees. And the freezer chest wasn't built for flying. Or landing.

I lay spreadeagled on top of it as it came crashing down through the trees, but it was heavier than me and there wasn't enough for me to hold on to. It fell faster than I did, the two of us coming apart as we hit an area where the trees were close together and the forest was a thick tangle. The outstretched branches pummelled the freezer chest, disturbing its flight path and sending it into a tumbling spin. I fell just behind it, colliding with a tree limb that hit my chest like a baseball bat, bruising my ribs and knocking the breath right out of me. I came to a very sudden stop and then dropped like a stone, crashing through the smaller branches. There wasn't even time to grab hold of anything as I fell, my face and hands burning from the scratches and cuts that were opening up all over my skin.

I hit the ground face down, with a painful crunch, and skidded on my front as the freezer disappeared from view, twisting and tumbling and crashing into the trees.

The helicopter passed overhead, its rhythmic thumping fading into the distance until it was nothing more than a faint heartbeat, then it was gone. The forest was silent except for the trickle of pine needles dropping in my wake, and the sound of my own breathing. There was a gash on my cheek, my ribs were bruised, my skin was scratched and cut all over, and every muscle was sore, but I had survived.

I sat up and looked about in a daze. 'Holy crap. I'm alive.'

What made it even more incredible was that my right hand was still bunched into a tight fist, gripping the handle of my knife – and the bow and arrows were still secure across my back.

My arms and legs complained when I tried to stand, and my face stung from the cut. Blood ran down my cheek and neck, and my whole body was racked with pain, but I pushed myself to my feet and took the bow from my back.

'Still in one piece,' I whispered as I checked it over. 'That's a miracle.' I looked up, seeing nothing but the mist, and shouted to the forest: 'Thank you!'

The fact that the bow and arrows were safe and that I had managed to separate the freezer chest from the helicopter could mean only one thing. I was right about the president being my trophy, and something in the forest was protecting me, encouraging me to take what it was offering.

There wasn't much time, though. It wouldn't take Hazar long to realize the president was gone, so the helicopter would be back any moment. I had to find that freezer chest first.

With stiff legs, I stumbled in the direction of the muddy bank I had spotted from the air. The eerie mist hung in the trees around me as if I was running through an alien world, but I knew where I was going and I knew it was close. I pushed on through the forest, struggling to stay on my feet as I brushed aside stray branches, wading through dense bracken until I burst out of the trees.

It was a relief to be in the open and see the muddy bank just ahead of me, a long, dark smear running from left to right, shrouded in mist. Inclining away from me, the bank sloped upwards six or seven metres, then appeared to fall away into an abyss on the other side. There was no way of knowing what was over the ridge. It might have been a gentle hill or a terrifying drop off the side of the mountain.

'President?' I called as I moved out on to the mud. 'President?'

Nothing.

'President?'

In the distance, the sound of the helicopter slipped into range. Hazar was coming back.

'President!' I shouted, feeling my sense of urgency grow. The mist might hide us from view, but if they came low enough, the twirling blades would clear it away and they would spot us. And what about the president's satellites? Could they see through mist?

'President?' I had to find him before they came back.

Slipping and sliding, I forgot about my aches and pains and scrambled across the mud, looking this way and that, searching for the white box.

'President?'

Then I saw a long, flat path scraped through the dark mud. The freezer chest must have landed here and shot up the gentle bank towards the tipping-off point. I set off towards it without delay, moving as quickly as I could, following the flattened trail of the freezer. The soft, wet ground squelched and sucked at my feet, so I bent forward, putting my hands on my knees to force my legs to work harder. There was almost no grip on the incline and my boots were becoming heavy with thick mud, making it difficult to move, but I battled on, slowly making my way higher.

Coming closer to the top, I began to hear another sound competing with the noise of the approaching helicopter. From somewhere nearby came the rush of cascading water.

Of course! The river.

We must be close to Lake Tuonela. As we came down, the trees had obscured it from view, but it made sense for it to be near here, and that noise was the river that fed it. It ran fast and white and fell into the lake in a frothing storm of tons and tons of water.

I stopped.

If the freezer had gone over the edge of this bank, it might have slipped all the way down the other side into the river. It might have splashed into the fast-moving water and washed down towards the waterfall. There was no way the president could survive that. He'd drown for sure.

'President!'

With a new surge of energy, I pushed harder and harder, struggling to the top of the incline where I stood looking down at the raging river. It rushed through the mist, flanked by mud and rocks and decaying driftwood, stopping for nothing and nobody.

And there, upside down on the riverbank, just a few paces from the water, was the large white freezer chest.

'President!'

I started to run, but without any grip my feet skidded out from beneath me, whipping backwards so that I landed on my stomach and carried on down the slope like I was lying face-forwards on a toboggan. Thick, slimy mud gathered in heaps around my shoulders and piled up in my face as I went. By the time I came to a stop, my mouth was full of it and my clothes and boots were caked in it. The weight of the mud meant that it took a lot of effort to get to my feet, but I struggled on, wiping my face and spitting out the grime as I shambled over to the president's prison.

The freezer was upside down and covered in muck and smears of my blood. Its corners were crushed in, and the sides were dented and scratched from its fall into the forest. I imagined how it must have felt for my friend to be trapped inside it, being tumbled about, not knowing what was happening. He must have been terrified – but as I came closer and saw the extent of the damage to the chest, I began to wonder if he could have survived his ordeal.

'Please don't be dead,' I whispered. 'Please don't be dead.'

Closer still, and the roar of the river filled my head, mingling with the beat of the approaching helicopter.

'Please don't be dead.'

When I reached the freezer chest, I put both hands on the side, dug my feet into the mud, and pushed as hard as I could to turn it. At first it refused to move, but with a little rocking and a bit more strength, I managed to tip it first on to its side, then upright.

I unlatched the old locking mechanism and threw open the lid.

The president was curled in the ice and bloody water at the bottom like a dead animal. He was battered and bruised, bleeding from his nose.

'President?' I whispered. 'Please don't be dead.'

He opened his eyes. 'Oskari?' Covered in mud as I was, I must have looked like some kind of forest creature. 'Is that you? What the hell just happened?'

'President!' I could hardly contain my excitement. 'You're alive!' I wanted to jump up and down, but there was no time for that. 'Come on, quick, let's get you out.'

'I don't know if I can move,' he mumbled.

'Of course you can. I'll help. Quick, before they come back.'

I reached into the chest and took his hands, helping him to sit up.

'I feel like I've been in a washing machine, not a freezer.'

'Anything broken?'

He shook his head. 'I don't think so.'

'I figured it out,' I said, unable to contain my excitement any longer. I had to tell him what I had realized; why our meeting was so important. 'I figured it out.'

'What? What are you . . .' He put his hands on his face and moaned. 'Oh my God. Everything hurts.'

'I know why I found you. I figured it out when I was up there.' I pointed to the sky as all the adrenaline of the past few minutes raged through me, lifting my exhilaration. 'The forest gives us each what we deserve. Those are the words. And it *did* give me something. Something big.'

The president looked at me like I wasn't making any sense.

'You.'

'What?'

'You. The President of the United States of America. That's what the forest gave me. *You*.'

'What? No . . .'

'Yes. And I listened to the trees, and I fought tooth and nail, and now I'm going to take you to my dad, and all my village will see.'

The president sighed and lay back down in the freezer. 'Why is everybody hunting me?'

I looked at him for a second, then reached in to grab him again. 'No, President, get up. We have to go. They're coming back.' I pointed at the sky as the thud of the helicopter began to drown out the sound of the river. 'Hazar and Morris are coming back.'

'I honestly don't think I can do this any more, Oskari. I'm beat.'

'No. We have to keep going. I have to save you. There's no one to help us. Instead of looking tough, we have to *be* tough.'

The president sat up and put his hands on his face. He rubbed hard, then looked up at me. 'Oskari, you're more of a man than anyone else I know.'

WATERFALL

'**W**e'll head back into the trees,' the president said as I helped him out of the freezer. 'They won't be able to find us in there, right? You can use your skills and—'

'It's too far.' I glanced back at the forest on the other side of the wide, muddy bank, and remembered how the men had slipped down from the helicopter on ropes. If they saw us running across the mud, it would be easy for them to drop down at the treeline and stop us. They would shoot me and capture the president.

'It's our only chance,' the president said, starting in that direction. 'Come on.'

'No.' I stopped him. 'Help me with this.' I grabbed his jacket and tugged at him, encouraging him to help me push the freezer towards the raging river. The froth was boiling at the banks, kicking cold spray into our faces.

He resisted, looking back at the trees, then turning to search the mist for the return of the helicopter.

'They're too close,' I shouted. 'We'll never make it before they get here.'

Always the helicopter. Always coming at us like a nightmare that wouldn't give up.

'But—'

'You said you believed in me! I've fought for you, tooth and nail, just like I'm supposed to. Like Hamara said. You have to help me with this. You're mine and I know what to do. Haven't I got you this far?'

He looked at me, grimacing with pain and doubt, then glanced back at the sky as the familiar thud of the helicopter grew louder and louder.

'All right,' he said. 'I'm in your hands.'

'Then push this into the water.' I put my shoulder to the freezer chest and dug my toes into the mud.

'My God, you want to use it like a boat?'

'No way,' I said. 'We'd never survive the waterfall in this. I have a better idea.'

'Waterfall?'

'Just help me get this in the river,' I shouted. 'It'll make us harder to find.'

Now the president seemed to understand what I wanted to do. If we left the freezer chest on the bank, Hazar and Morris might spot it from above – a white box lying in the dark mud – and it would make their job easier. If we put it in the river, it would disappear for ever.

186

It only took a couple of good shoves for us to get it right to the edge and tip it into the raging torrent. As soon as the water touched it, it skewed the box and snatched it away, dragging it into the main current. The freezer bobbed and spun as it raced along in the white water of the river, then it was gone.

'What now?' the president asked. 'Bury ourselves in the mud? Jump in?'

'Close,' I said. 'Come with me. I have a plan.'

We were both in a bad way, aching and hurt, but we supported each other as we stumbled along the river-bank, moving in the direction of the flowing water. Above, the helicopter circled, buzzing this way and that as it searched for us.

'We're lucky to have the mist,' the president said.

'The forest sent it,' I told him as we came off the mud on to a more solid part of the bank. There was thin grass here, and large rocks that funnelled the water towards the falls.

'You really think so?'

'Of course.' I had to shout over the noise of the river. It was getting louder all the time now, drowning out the searching helicopter, but the president didn't seem to notice, he was so deep in thought.

'Well, it's the only thing keeping us safe at the moment, but . . .' He shook his head and stopped.

'But what, President?' I encouraged him to keep going, moving forwards to our escape.

'Nothing.'

'Tell me,' I shouted.

'They have access to satellite feeds. I saw it on Morris's phone when we were on the mountain. It was right there on his screen, an aerial picture of him and me and the helicopter. If they have that, then they'll have access to thermal imaging, too. That means—'

'It means they can see our body heat, right? I've seen it on a video game.'

'Yeah, of course you have. Well, it means the mist won't help us, and that . . . oh my God.' The president stopped. '*This* is your plan?'

Just ahead, the riverbank disappeared. It fell away as if we had come to the end of the world and there was nothing more beyond it. Nowhere else to go. Squinting into the patchy mist, though, we could just about make out the surface of Lake Tuonela thirty or forty metres below.

'We're going to jump,' I shouted.

'No way!' The president tensed and started to turn back. 'No way!'

'It's fine.' I grabbed him and made him come with me to the edge and look down. There wasn't much to see, though, because the water spilled from the river, cascading over the black rocks, and disappeared into the sheet of mist that swirled below us.

'We can't jump over there, Oskari. We'll die.'

'No, we won't,' I said. 'I promise.'

I kept hold of his jacket and led him further along the cliff top, telling him to be careful not to slip on the rocks. We kept on, moving away from the main spout of the waterfall, until we came to a rocky ledge that jutted out across the lake, to the left of the place where the bulk of the river smashed into the surface below.

'It's safe to jump here,' I told him. 'Take off your jacket.'

'No way.' The president shook his head and limped back. 'I'd rather take my chances back there with them.'

'They'll kill you.' The noise of the water was like thunder, my voice almost lost to it.

'*This* will kill me. If *they* wanted to kill me, they would have done it already. I'll take my chances.'

'They'll kill *me*,' I shouted. As we spoke, I took the bow and quiver from my back before unfastening my camouflage netting and shrugging it off to the ground. I removed my jacket and took the fire kit from the pocket before throwing it to one side.

'They don't want you,' he said. 'They want me. If they get me, they'll forget about you.'

'They're not getting you,' I shouted at him as I secured the fire kit in the zip-up pocket of my hoodie. 'They're NOT getting you!' Crouching, I took out my knife and cut strips from my camouflage netting, twisting them into cords. 'Take off your jacket.'

'This is not a good idea, Oskari,' the president shouted in my ear.

'Trust me. I first jumped over these falls when I was five years old.' I put one of the cords around his waist and fastened it with a tight knot.

'What?' He looked stunned.

'I jumped with my dad. I've done it many times since.' I put a second cord around my own waist and secured it.

'Now, take off your jacket.'

'Many times?'

'Well . . . twice. But I know it's safe. I've seen lots of people do it. We *all* do it when we are five.'

'Are you people mad?'

'No! I told you – we have to be tough.'

'Well, you're right about that.'

I took the third cord and looped it around the one I had put on the president, slipping it under his belt for extra security.

'When my dad and I jumped,' I explained, 'we tied ourselves together like this so we couldn't be separated.' I put the other end of the third cord around my own and secured it with a good knot. 'If you don't take off your jacket, it will be more difficult for you.'

The president swallowed hard and fixed his eyes on mine. 'Well, I guess if you could do it when you were five . . .'

I jammed my knife back into the sheath on my belt and clipped the fastener before putting a hand on my pocket to check that my fire kit was still there. With that done, I collected the bow and quiver, making sure they were secure. I had everything I needed to survive.

'And you *really* did this when you were five?' he asked, slipping out of his jacket and throwing it down into the lake where it wouldn't be found.

'Yes, really. Now jump!'

With that, I shoved him hard over the edge, and threw myself after him.

IN THE DEPTHS

The cord pulled tight between us as we dropped and dropped. The wind rushed around me, cold and fierce. It forced its way into my nostrils and open mouth, filling my lungs with its freshness until I thought I might burst. The spray from the falls made it feel as if I was tumbling through rain, and the sound of wind and water was deafening, but it was only a few seconds before I hit the lake.

I struck it with force, like an explosion in my ears as I plunged into the water and sank. The falls pushed me deeper into the cold darkness, frothing around me, disorientating me. It was impossible to know which way was up and which was down. The cord around my waist tightened further as the president was washed in a different direction, and my chest began to heave for breath. I had to get to the surface, but I didn't know which way to go. I kicked out in panic, my legs heavy with sodden jeans and boots, starting to think maybe this had been a bad mistake. We shouldn't have jumped. It was a mistake, and now we were going to die down here, drowned in the lake beneath the torrent of the waterfall.

I twisted and turned, looking for the surface, surrounded by bubbles and rock and current. Kicking towards what I thought was the surface, there was a sudden jolt as the bow jammed against the rocks behind me. Panic rose higher and higher. I had to get free.

I tried to go down, wriggling to loosen the bow, and when I did, the weight of the water caught me again, pushing me deeper.

My chest was burning now. All my breath was gone, and my vision was beginning to darken. All I could think about was the *näkki* lurking in the depths below, watching me with those staring, yellow eyes. I imagined it reaching up with its writhing tentacles, curling them around my feet and dragging me down. I was five years old again, terrified of the monster in the lake, kicking out in horror. I wanted to open my mouth, to draw air into my body, but there was no air to be had. Panic was coursing through me, telling me to take a breath; telling me I would have to open my mouth soon, but I knew that if I did – *when* I did – all I would suck into my lungs would be water. And that would be the end. It was just as I had imagined that first time, when I had jumped with Dad. The *näkki* would take me and I was going to die.

In my fight against the powerful current of the waterfall, I didn't notice the cord pulling at my waist. As my flailing arms and legs weakened, and my world began to die, I didn't notice that I was already moving through the water.

Then I was rising. Up and up. Bubbles boiled around me.

It was Dad. He was pulling me up. Of course he was. Dad, who was so strong. Dad, who had killed the bear. Dad, who had dragged me up to the surface when I was five years old. He was saving me again, pulling me out of the water to take me home to Mum.

Hands on me now, grabbing the hood of my sweater, dragging me up and out of the water.

I broke the surface with an explosion, bursting out and opening my mouth wide. I gasped for air, sucking it deep into my lungs, overwhelmed by the relief and exhilaration of still being alive.

'Dad!' I said, looking around, light-headed and confused. 'Dad?'

'Just me, Oskari.'

The president was beside me, holding my hood with both hands, treading water. His chin was touching the surface of the lake, small waves lapping at his face, and he spat water from his mouth. 'Thought it was game over, eh?'

'The bow got stuck. I couldn't swim up.' Faint, lingering memories of Mum and Dad, and the slithering tentacles of the *näkki*, reeled in my head, giving me a strange sense of disappointment and discomfort that mingled with the joy of having survived.

'Didn't I tell you to get rid of it? Make a smaller one?'

'I have to—'

'I know, I know.'

We floated side by side, treading water, and I looked at him. 'Thank you,' I said. 'For saving me.'

'I guess we've got each other's backs.'

'Yeah. Pretty cool, wasn't it?'

'Cool? You almost drowned.'

'I know,' I said, and began to laugh. I couldn't explain it. I guess I was just happy to be alive, and the president must have sensed that, too, because he couldn't help smiling and then laughing along with me. If anybody could have seen us, they would have thought we were lunatics.

Our laughter was short-lived, though, because as we swam away from the drag of the waterfall, we heard the helicopter descending over the lake and circling above us, hidden by the mist.

'They know we're here,' the president said.

'Thermal imaging?' I asked.

'Could be. Either that or they're guessing.'

I used my knife to sever the cord that joined us together, and we swam deeper into the mist. 'There are small islands in the lake,' I said as we slipped through the calmer water. 'If we can get to one of those—'

'If they have thermal imaging, no island is going to help us.'

'But we have to take that chance, right? What else can we do?'

'Pray?'

GHOST IN THE MIST

We might have been swimming in circles for all we knew. Everything looked the same. Water, water and more water. The mist hid us from the circling helicopter, but it also hid everything else from view, and we couldn't swim for shore or for one of the lake islands if we couldn't see them. It was difficult to move, laden down as we were with our clothes, and the water was cold, making us sluggish. If we didn't get out soon, we'd probably freeze or drown anyway, and Hazar and Morris could stop looking.

'What time do you think it is?' the president asked as we swam side by side. 'My watch stopped.'

'Nine-thirty.' I squinted into the sky, searching for the helicopter.

'That some kind of hunter thing?' he asked. 'You can tell by looking at the sun?'

'Can't see the sun.' I lifted my left wrist. 'I have a waterproof watch, though.'

The president spat out a mouthful of lake water. 'Nine-thirty, eh? I should be in a conference right now, sitting on my ass drinking coffee. Saving the world.'

'It'll have to wait.'

We kept on swimming, finding a slow rhythm as we pushed on through the water. Although we couldn't see the helicopter through the mist, and the echo across the calm lake made it difficult to pinpoint, it seemed to be coming closer and closer to our position.

'You think they know where we are?' I asked.

'I don't know. Maybe whoever's looking at those satellite feeds and giving them directions can't see us for some reason. Maybe the thermal imaging's no good because we're so damn cold and not giving off much of a signature, who knows? I should have paid more attention to satellite stuff, I guess.'

The thought of all those cameras up there, looking down at us from beyond the clouds, had a strange effect on me. I felt like a goldfish in a bowl; as if there was nowhere I could go to get away from those prying eyes. I was thinking about what thermal imaging looked like in video games and on TV, and I was seeing us in those pictures – a grey landscape, with two tiny white bodies, glowing as we swam about as if in mid-air. I hoped the president was right, and that the cold water was lowering our body temperature and making us hard to spot, but the problem was that it was also making it harder and harder to keep going.

'I'm getting tired.' I was exhausted and wasn't sure how much longer I could keep swimming.

'Me, too, but don't stop. Whatever you do, don't stop.'

I knew why he'd said it. If we stopped, the cold and tiredness would seize and cramp our muscles, and that would be the end of it. We'd sink into the darkness and disappear. So, while the helicopter searched from above, we pushed on and on through the mist and water as if we would be swimming for ever, until hope came in the shape of an unexpected object floating on the lake.

'Look,' I said, trying to lift my head out of the water to see better. 'What's that?' It was a few metres ahead of us, unclear in the mist. 'Is that . . .? It is! The freezer!'

With a renewed burst of speed, we swam towards the chest and grabbed hold, giving ourselves a much-needed break. As soon I stopped, though, everything hurt. I hadn't thought about it when I was swimming, but now all the cuts and scratches on my skin stung, and my muscles ached.

'We can't stop,' the president said, so we held on to the chest, side by side, and began kicking, pushing it through the water, resting from time to time. 'Oskari, how big *is* this lake?'

'Big,' I said. 'But we should have found something by now.' I stopped kicking, lifted my face to the wind and breathed deeply. 'What's that smell?'

The president stopped, too, and wiped his face before sniffing. He turned around, looking in all directions.

'Gasoline? Some kind of fuel?'

'That's what it smells like to me.'

'Fumes from the helicopter?'

'No, this smells different. Stronger.'

As I spoke, something caught my attention as it floated past. Something silver, flashing, bobbing up and down on the surface of the lake. I reached out and splashed at the water, making the object drift close enough for me to grab and hold up for us to look at.

'A fish?' the president said.

'Looks like roach,' I told him, seeing how the light caught its scales. It shimmered green and blue and red, just like a drop of petrol on the surface of a puddle. 'This lake is full of roach. Bream and perch, too.'

'Is it dead? What killed it?'

I shook my head and watched in wonder as more fish drifted out of the mist, flickering on the gentle waves. At first there were just one or two of them, then more and more slipped past until we were surrounded by dead fish. There were hundreds of them, glittering and sparkling on the surface of Lake Tuonela.

'What *is* this?' The president spun around, staring at all the silvery bodies bobbing up and down.

'There's something in the water,' I said, rubbing my fingers together, feeling the oiliness of the lake. I could taste it on my lips, too. 'Some kind of fuel.' I could see it now, shimmering across the surface in a rainbow of colours wherever it caught the light. The surface of the lake was covered with fuel. 'Where's it coming from?'

'Right there.'

As we drifted forwards, a huge white-and-blue tail loomed out of the swirling mist in front of us.

It was bigger than my house, straight and sharp, cutting up into the air like a knife. On the side of it, printed in bold colours, was the American flag.

'That's my plane,' the president said. 'That's Air Force One.'

I stared in disbelief as we kicked closer, steering the freezer chest forwards to see the rest of the giant aeroplane outlined in the mist like a ghost.

'It must have skimmed across the water.' The president looked behind us as if he expected to see some kind of trail. 'Been here all night. I wonder why it hasn't sunk.'

Coming closer, though, we could see why. The plane must have landed on the lake, just like the president said, and had skimmed across the surface until it collided with one of the small islands. The nose was wedged at a slight angle in the shallows, pointing towards the silver birch that grew there. The rest of the enormous plane was sitting back in the water, so the engines were completely submerged. Part of the tail was beneath the water, too, and the blue stripe that ran the length of the plane disappeared beneath the lake halfway along its body.

'It's massive.' I stopped kicking and shook my head, unable to take my eyes off it. 'My *village* isn't even that long.'

'And it's twenty metres high, which makes it like a six-storey building.'

'Air Force One.' I clung to the freezer and let my legs hang still in the water, swaying with the gentle current.

'It's massive,' I said again. 'And it's all yours?'

'Well, kind of.' He stared at the plane and shook his head. 'There were a lot of people on board. Not a full crew, but . . .' He let his words trail away.

I tore my eyes from the plane and turned to look at the president, seeing the pain in his expression. 'Maybe they're okay?' I said, but I didn't really believe it. Half the plane was under water, and there was a long black scorch mark reaching up from beneath the near wing. It stretched right over the back of the plane, and I guessed it had something to do with those missiles I had seen streaking up into the sky last night.

'Shot down,' the president said. 'Just like you told me.' He took a deep breath and puffed his cheeks as he blew it out. 'The front section is above the water – maybe some of them managed to get to safety.'

His words were almost drowned out by the thudding of the helicopter as it buzzed overhead. The sound didn't recede, though; instead it continued, right above us, then it began to descend, buffeting the water and sending large ripples ever outwards from our position.

I looked up to see the dark shape coming closer, the haziness of the rotor blades as the main body of the helicopter became more solid and the mist whipped away.

'Damn it,' the president shouted. 'Won't they ever give up?'

Ropes dropped from the helicopter, falling into the water beside me.

'Tip this over!' he shouted.

'What?'

'Tip this over!'

It took a second for me to understand what he meant, but as soon as I did, we flipped the freezer chest over so it was upside down in the water, the lid hanging down into the lake.

The ropes quivered and I glanced up to see legs and boots appear from the side of the helicopter, then Hazar's men were rappelling down towards us, weapons ready.

'Dive!' the president shouted, and we sank under the surface, coming up inside the pocket of air trapped in the freezer.

'Now what?' I said, treading water in the darkness. 'Any ideas?'

The president spat water and breathed heavily, but said nothing.

'What about the plane?' My voice sounded flat inside the box. 'Can we get inside without them seeing us?'

'Maybe. I don't know.'

Something moved above us, knocking against the freezer. A rope, perhaps, or maybe it was something else. Boots. Or hands.

'They're going to get us any moment,' I said. *'Can we get inside the plane?'*

'I don't know!' he shouted back. 'I don't know, Oskari.'

'Then we have to try. Come on, President, we have a plane to catch.'

As the freezer chest began to lift away from us, we dived down into the lake and headed for the plane.

ANOTHER WORLD

The sound of the helicopter was deadened into a dull, repetitive thump, and the surface rippled above like a moving ceiling. The enormous monster that was Air Force One listed towards us, one wing cutting down into the lake, bubbles rising around it. Its huge bulk hung above the darkness below. It looked as if all it would take was a small push and the whole plane would slide backwards and disappear into the cold depths, a place that my imagination filled with terrifying tentacled creatures and monsters with grasping claws.

I tried not to think about such things as I swam hard and fast towards Air Force One.

Here and there, sections of the plane glowed in the

gloom, shafts of light shimmering from the windows and diffusing into the murky water. Red and green and orange, flickering on and off, reminding me of how I had thought the president's escape pod held an alien when I first saw it in the trees.

We passed the wing, where one engine hung useless, dangling over the abyss. The second engine was completely gone, shredded right off by the missile, leaving a tear in the underside of the wing and a black scar that reached up to the back of the plane.

There was a gaping hole in the fuselage, too, right behind the wing, so the president led me that way, past the twisted metal edges and into the plane. We surfaced immediately in a small pocket of air and I tried to stay calm, to control my breathing, but it was difficult not to be afraid. The thought of becoming trapped here and drowning in the lake kept sliding through my mind like a cold eel.

'Was it a good idea?' I asked, hoping the answer was 'yes.'

'I don't know yet. We're in the secretarial area right now, but it should be dry in my suite and at the upper deck.' The president's voice was deadened by the cramped breathing space.

'Can we get to it?' I battled away the creeping feeling of dread.

'Maybe, but there's still a little way to go.'

'Will it be clear?' I didn't want to drown down there, where no one would ever find me. Dad would never know what had happened to me, and he would be left to search the forest for ever.

'I hope so. Follow me.'

'Okay,' I said, and we dived back under, forging our way deeper into the belly of the plane.

Swimming through the plane's corridors was horrible and otherworldly. Strip lights on the floor and ceiling shone a dull, red glow through the water as if it was tinged with blood. They flickered on and off, sometimes with a sudden flash of green or orange that blinked for an instant and then was gone. Objects floated in slow motion, swaying in the lazy current. Bags and papers and cases drifted through Air Force One, seeming to hang in mid-air. A shoe. A jacket, billowing like a jelly-fish. A cushion heading at me from the darkness beyond the lights and slipping past like a strange prehistoric animal. Doors swayed open and closed, giving shocking glimpses of men and women still buckled into their seats, arms drifting in the current, hair washing about like weeds. There were other shapes, too, just out of sight, bobbing around like monsters waiting in the shadows.

Coming up to breathe whenever possible, we took a few moments to suck the stale air into our lungs before diving under again and pushing on through the floating debris. We swam deeper and deeper into the plane, moving up through corridors filled with snowstorms of papers, and squeezing through doorways. The tilted and twisted position of the plane skewed everything at an awkward angle, confusing me and scrambling my sense of direction. Sometimes it was hard to know which way was up and which was down, and in places the water was so laden with floating wreckage that my bow snagged, slowing me down, so I took it from my back and swam with it gripped in one hand.

Every time I took another breath and dived down, I had the feeling it would be my last; that eventually we would come to a dead end, and everything would go black, and we would suck water into our lungs and cough out our last hope of living.

'Almost there,' the president said when we came up for breath.

I looked at him in the dim light and nodded without saying anything.

'You all right?' he asked.

I nodded again.

'Pretty scary, isn't it?'

'Yes.'

'Well, it's not far now. Ready?'

I took a deep breath and was about to nod again, when something brushed against my leg. Without thinking I kicked out and splashed away from it, backing into the president in my panic. A million horrible images flashed through my head, of monsters in the water, of those shadowy shapes just out of sight.

'It's all right,' the president was saying. 'It's all right.' But I hardly heard him. Blood was thumping in my ears and I was trying to get away from whatever it was, splashing in the water, making it chop in the small breathing space.

'Get it off me,' I said as I backed into him. 'Get it off!'

I pressed him against the wall, fighting to escape, releasing my grip on the bow.

And then it showed its face.

The body bobbed up beside me, breaking the surface of the water with a gentle plop.

The woman's eyes were open, staring right at me, but she was dead. There was a dark hole in her forehead, clean and without any blood, because it had washed away in the water. Her hair floated around her head like it was alive, swishing this way and that in the current.

'Don't look at her,' the president said, taking hold of me. 'Don't look.'

I turned around to face him, unable to get the image out of my mind, knowing she was right behind me.

'Just breathe,' the president said. 'Breathe and calm down. It's not far now. The galley is along here, and there are stairs to the upper deck.'

'Do you know her?' I asked when I started to calm down. 'Is she . . .?'

'Her name was Patricia Young. She was on my staff. We're in the senior staff area.'

'That hole. She was shot?'

'Yeah. I think you might be right. I guess Morris did a thorough job of covering his tracks.' The president held on to me. 'You ready to go again?'

'I dropped my bow.'

'Leave it.'

'I can't.'

'You don't need it.'

'I have to find it.' Suddenly it was the only thing that

mattered; the only thing connecting me to home and to Dad. I looked down into the dark water. 'You see it?'

'Leave it, Oskari. You'll—'

I dived down, feeling in the darkness. The dead woman washed against me, her legs brushing my body as I grasped for the bow, and I gritted my teeth. I had to find it. It was my duty to take it home.

I spun in the water, waving my hands around me, hoping beyond hope that I would find it. I grabbed at anything and everything. My fingers touched each object they encountered, checking them and discarding them until . . . there. At the bottom of the cabin, snagged on something . . .

I came up for air, disturbing the body once again, then went back down, finding the bow and working it free. One end of it was trapped under some kind of chair that must have shifted when I panicked, so I wedged my shoulders against the wall and used my feet to shove it. The chair resisted at first, then gave way, and the bow was free, floating away from me. I whipped around and grasped it tight before pushing to the surface, bursting out of the water.

'Got it.' I held the bow out for the president to see.

'You ready now?' he asked.

I moved away from him and nodded. 'Let's get this over with.'

We took a deep breath and went under again, only this time I knew what those dark shapes beyond the lights were: they were the bodies of the people who had been in the plane, and there were more of them here. Men and women drifting in a tangle, floating among the papers and pens and lost shoes.

Their arms seemed to reach out for us as we swam past.

AIR FORCE ONE

We didn't stop to rest when we finally dragged ourselves out of the water. The feeling that Hazar and Morris were right behind us kept us pressing on.

'This way,' the president said, and I followed, trudging along the corridor, water pouring from my clothes on to the beige carpet. Around us, the plane groaned and creaked as if it was preparing to die.

We passed a meeting room strewn with chairs and files, with a large oval table fixed in the centre. There might have been a pair of legs protruding from beneath the table, but I looked away and fixed my eyes on the president's back as he led me through a large, heavy door. When we were both on the other side of it, he sealed the door behind us and locked it shut.

'We should be safe in here.' The president wiped his face and ran his hands along each arm to squeeze some of the water from his shirtsleeves. 'Even if they come into the plane, they'll never get through this door. It's designed to keep terrorists out.' He forced a smile at me. 'You're on my turf now, Oskari.'

I nodded and copied what he was doing, trying to wring some of the lake out of my clothes.

'That's the galley in there.' The president pointed to the room on my left. 'The medical office and my suite are just back here.' He pointed over his shoulder. 'These stairs lead up to the comms centre and the flight deck. Come on.'

I flicked water from my hands as I followed him, glancing into the medical office and bumping into the president when he stopped in front of me.

'This is our way out,' he said, putting a hand on the door to our left. The large exit was set into the wall of the aircraft, with a red handle to one side of it. The words TURN TO OPEN were printed around it.

'We can open it from in here and get out if we need to.' The president looked down at me. 'Have you ever seen the President of the United States coming out of Air Force One? Waving to the crowds?'

I shook my head.

'Never seen *that* on TV?'

I shook my head again.

'Well.' He sighed. 'If you ever did, it's this door he comes out of – *I* come out of. Should've been coming out of it this morning.' He paused. 'Anyway, first things first. This way.' He pushed open the door to his right and we walked through into his office.

'You ever been in the White House, Oskari?'

'No.'

'Well, you have now. If I'm in this room, it's the White House.'

The dark wooden desk, set across the far corner, was still fixed in place, but there was nothing on top of it. The papers, files, and laptop that had probably been there were now strewn across the brown carpet or piled on the leather corner couch that was opposite. The president's office chair was there, too, wheels turned up towards the ceiling like a dead animal. A curtain was pulled back along the far wall revealing a blue-and-gold presidential seal and a row of five porthole windows. The blinds were all down, letting in only a few cracks of white light. The whole place smelled of wood and leather and polish.

'Have a look over there.' The president pointed at the couch. 'See if you can find my cell phone; this one's ruined.' He pulled the bodyguard's phone from his pocket and threw it aside as he hurried over to the desk and began yanking out drawers. Above him was a small opening in the ceiling, with a plastic tube hanging down like a thread of spider silk. On the end of it was a yellow face mask that swung and jiggled about when he bumped into it. There were more masks just like it close to me, hanging from the ceiling above the corner couch.

I rummaged through the papers and files, throwing them on to the floor behind me until I spotted a black smartphone wedged between two of the seat cushions. 'Here!'

'Well done.' The president came around his desk and took it from me. He switched it on and waited for the screen to light up. 'Surprise, surprise,' he said. 'No signal.' He held it up and turned around a few times, then threw it on to the floor and kicked the desk. 'Damn it! Why don't I have a satellite phone like that traitor Morris?'

'You have any other ideas?' I asked.

'Right.' He rubbed his face. 'What now? Think, think, think. Ah! Upstairs. Comms centre and flight deck. If there's any chance of calling for help, it'll be up there.' He turned and hurried from the room. 'Come on, Oskari.'

We made our way back along the corridor and climbed the stairs into the communications centre where, despite the angle of the plane, the desks were still in place, fixed against the walls to our left and right. Everything else was a mess. Above the desks were large banks of charred electronic equipment, with every screen cracked, as if damaged deliberately. There were pieces of broken plastic and wires hanging out of them like entrails. Five large office chairs and other pieces of ruined electronic equipment were lying against the left wall, covering what looked like more bodies, and the floor was littered with loose papers and wires and laptops with their screens smashed. Yellow oxygen masks dangled from the ceiling, gently swaying from side to side. A tangy smell hung in the air, mixed with a hint of burning.

The president stopped in front of me and looked around. He put one hand on the wall to support himself and shook his head in disbelief. 'No chance of using any of this to call for help.'

'But how are the lights still on?' I asked.

'Emergency power, I guess. This is no ordinary plane. The hull is ten times stronger than a civilian passenger jet. It's designed to withstand a nuclear blast on the ground – all the windows are armoured, it has enemy radar jamming, flares to confuse enemy missiles, infrared to confuse enemy guidance systems—'

'So how did someone shoot it down?'

The president raised his eyebrows. 'That's a good question, Oskari, and there's only one answer I can think of. Morris. He must have sabotaged the systems. There were twenty-six crew members on this plane. My security detail, staff members . . . more than forty people in total, and he just . . . threw them away like that. A man who I thought was my friend. Maybe he was right – maybe the president can't have friends.'

'I'm your friend,' I said.

'Yes, you are. And you've proved it often enough. Come on, flight deck's this way, maybe we'll have better luck there.' He stepped past the debris and went through the door into the next room, saying, 'crew lounge,' but I kept my eyes on his back, not wanting to see any more bodies as I followed him to the far end and entered the cockpit.

I thought it would need a massive flight deck to fly a beast like this, but it was actually quite cramped. There was enough room for a small table with a couple of chairs behind the pilot's and co-pilot's seats, but that was it.

The nose of the plane was raised slightly because it was resting on the shallows of the small island, so the curved window gave us a good view of the surface of the lake on either side. Over to our left I could just about make out the shore, but it didn't look like much more than a dark strip from here.

'You think we could make it over there before they spot us?' I asked.

'Might be worth a try.'

The mist still hung over the water, but was a little thinner than before. There was a growing brightness that suggested the sun was trying to come out and burn it away, so maybe it would be gone by midday. I imagined the sky would be blue this afternoon, with just the slightest wisp of cloud. I wasn't sure we'd live long enough to see it, though.

There was the same tangy, smoky stink of burned-out electronics in here as there had been in the communications centre, and a variety of insistent pinging and beeping noises pulsed every few seconds. The alarms sounded in a chorus that fell in time with some of the lights flickering around the cockpit.

The president went straight to the front, standing between the pilot and co-pilot's seats, leaning in to look at the array of equipment. There was a baffling assortment of switches and dials and screens and buttons. Some of them were dead, but others were alight, flashing as if they were expecting attention.

'Gotta be something here,' he said. 'There has to be a radio or *something*.' He scanned the dials and buttons, touching this and that, shaking his head. 'How the hell do they ever learn what all these are?'

He leaned closer, putting his hand on the throttle. Right away, the plane heaved and started to shake as if the engines were trying to start up. A warning siren began to scream, filling the flight deck, and a series of red lights erupted on the instrument panel.

The president jumped back in shock, releasing the lever. The lights stopped flashing, the siren stopped screaming and the plane stopped shuddering.

He put one hand on the back of the pilot's seat and the other on his chest. 'Damn. Almost gave me a heart attack.' He turned to look at me. 'Incredible. It's like there's still power to the engines. They always told me it's designed to withstand impacts that would obliterate a normal plane.'

'I guess people aren't designed to withstand the same impacts.' I pointed my chin towards the front of the seat, and he looked down to see the pilot lying in a heap on the floor.

The president took a jacket from beside the co-pilot's chair and draped it over the dead man.

I turned away and looked out of the window, watching the lake rippling a few metres below the level of the glass to my left. There was something about it that bothered me.

'Did you find a radio?' I asked. 'Is there anything we

can use to call for help?'

The president looked at me for a long moment, then shook his head. 'Truth is, I don't know how any of this stuff works, Oskari.'

'What are we going to do, then? What do we do now?'

He sat on the edge of the pilot's seat so our faces were level, and he put his hands on my shoulders. 'Look at me,' he said, making me turn to meet his eyes. 'We're going to make it, Oskari.'

'How?'

'All we have to do is sit tight and wait for the military to arrive. They must have found us by now.'

'Using their satellites?'

He nodded.

'The same ones Morris is using?'

'Most probably.'

I turned and looked out of the window again, watching the water. Something wasn't right. I leaned closer, peering down and frowning.

'What is it?' the president asked, getting to his feet. 'You see something?'

'It's getting higher,' I said. 'The water.'

'No, it can't—' He pressed in beside me and looked down.

'President, I think we're sinking. I don't think we can wait here much longer.'

But there was something else about the water, too. As we watched, the mist swirled around like a tornado and the movement on the surface grew larger and more troubled, buffeting more and more until a large ripple formed. The way it looked reminded me of the time a rock had bounced up and hit Dad's windscreen. The glass had stayed in one piece, but had cracked in a circular pattern, with a hole in the middle and a thousand tiny fractures running away from it. That's what the lake looked like now.

'Helicopter?' I whispered.

A vibration shook through the plane – not violent like it had been when the president touched the controls, but a gentle shaking.

'Yeah.' The president nodded. 'But whose? The military's, or Morris's?'

The vibration continued to shake through the plane as other eerie sounds echoed in the cockpit, making us both look up at the ceiling. There was a rasping and shuffling of something being dragged across the top of the fuselage, then a strange metallic scraping noise followed by two heavy thuds.

'Someone's on the roof.' My voice was barely audible, my throat tightening in fear. 'You think it's your soldiers?' The unmistakable noise of boots clomping just above us resonated through the flight deck. 'Navy SEALs?'

The president didn't answer. He just shook his head and continued to look at the ceiling, as if doing it for long enough might give him X-ray vision.

The footsteps moved right over our heads towards the front of the plane.

'I don't like it . . .' the president said.

I didn't like it, either, and I turned my head, following the noises until they stopped above the pilot's seat. 'Sounds like two sets of boots to me.'

'Just two?'

I nodded and glanced at the president. Just two sets. We both knew what that meant. And to confirm our worst fears, a face appeared at the top of the window, upside down, peering into the cockpit.

Morris.

There was a look of surprise when he first saw us, then he locked eyes with the president and grinned. In that moment, he looked like a devil, eyes glinting with victory. He tilted his head a touch and waggled his fingers before disappearing from view.

The next thing we saw was Morris's hand, swinging down hard to stick a lump of what looked like putty to the window.

The president reacted right away, grabbing my arm and dragging me back towards the door. 'Explosives!' he shouted. 'Get out of here!'

NO WAY OUT

The president shoved me out of the flight deck ahead of him, sending me barrelling into the crew lounge, crashing into one of the beds on my right. I tripped, falling to one knee, but the president grabbed me and pulled me to my feet.

'Keep going!' he shouted. 'Get out! Get out!' He pushed me on, yanking the door shut behind him and yelling at me to move faster as we raced through the communications centre and headed for the stairs.

We only made it down the first few steps before the explosion ripped through the upper deck of Air Force One.

For a heartbeat, all the air was sucked out of the world. My lungs deflated, a piercing jolt flashed through my head and my eyes felt as if they were swelling in my skull. My ears deadened when the sound reached them, and every single one of my joints popped and screamed out in pain. Then the plane shuddered as pressure and heat raced after us like a demon.

A solid wall of force rushed through the cockpit, bringing a mess of shrapnel and debris with it, a raging cloud of destruction that smashed through the crew lounge, singeing everything it touched. The communications centre door gave way under its power, blasting inwards and allowing the energy to fill that room, too, collecting pieces of broken glass and plastic and burning paper as it went.

We were halfway down the stairs when the force of the explosion reached us. By then it had lost much of its intensity, but it still snatched us off our feet and threw us to the corridor below, where we landed on the damp beige carpet in a disorganized heap. Fragments from the crew lounge and the communications centre bombarded us, hammering the ground like heavy rain on leaves.

Straight away, I tried to get up, but nothing seemed to work properly. My legs were like soft rubber and my arms were shaking. My vision was hazy and I could hardly think.

The plane filled with hot smoke, and there was an awful smell of burning and charred plastic that stung my eyes and caught in the back of my throat, making me cough. I put a hand over my mouth and made myself stop, afraid that it would give us away even though all I could hear was a high-pitched whining in my ears.

I turned my head in slow motion, the world swimming in front of me as I reeled from the effects of the shockwave. The president was lying beside me, trying to focus, but his eyes were streaming and rolling about. He reached out to reassure me and we stayed still, side by side, trying to recover.

'—after us,' the president said.

'What?' I tried to sit up and lean closer. I rubbed my face with both hands, then stuck my fingers in my ears and waggled them about, feeling some sense of normality return.

'I said, they're coming after us.'

'Should we go back?' With some effort, I turned to glance at the security door, half-hidden by smoke, and shivered at the thought of trying to make it back through the plane, the way we had come.

'Too risky. We're already sinking.' The president coughed. 'We both saw that. Maybe the air pockets are gone.' He paused to wipe his irritated eyes. 'We were lucky we found what we did when we came through. This whole plane's going to be under water soon. That explosion has only made it worse.'

'The side door, then. The one you wave from.'

The president got to his feet and put a hand on the wall to steady himself as he looked along the corridor. Tears streamed down his cheeks and he squeezed his eyes shut over and over again, trying to wash away the effects of the acrid smoke. 'They'll just come after us. They're never going to stop, Oskari. Never.' He shook his head. 'They don't want to kill me, though, not yet. Hazar said he wants to . . .'

I remembered what Hazar had said about stuffing the president and displaying him. It was too horrible to even think about.

He looked at me with a serious expression. 'I think maybe it's time to give myself up.'

He was a wreck. His shoulders were hunched and he could hardly stand up straight. His eyes were bloodshot and streaming with tears, and his body hitched as he coughed the smoky atmosphere out of his lungs. His skin was covered with cuts and bruises and scrapes; he looked like a beaten man. I would have bet anything that I looked beaten too, and the obvious thing was to give up. We were outnumbered, outgunned, and backed into a corner with almost no way out.

But I had the blood of hunters in my veins.

I had one day and one night to find out what kind of a man I was. I had to know how to listen and fight tooth and nail for my prey. Nothing would be given to me for free.

Hamara's words.

A boy set out into the wilderness, but a man would return.

I frowned at the president. 'No.'

'What?'

'I said "No". I have the blood of hunters in my veins.'

'It's over, Oskari. We're finished. We've had enough. You can escape when I'm gone — get out of the door I showed you.' The plane lurched beneath us as he spoke, throwing us against the wall. 'I'll tell them you're dead.'

'No,' I said again, feeling the fear begin to slip away. I *had* had enough, but that didn't mean I was going to run away. The time for running was gone. I was moving beyond fear now, and my instincts were changing.

'Mr President!' Hazar's voice echoed through the upper deck and floated down the hazy stairwell. 'Where are you, Mr President?'

We looked at each other, but the cold tightness that had gripped my insides was no longer as firm.

'Mr President?' The sing-song voice snaked through the smoke. 'Don't make me come looking for you.'

'I have to give myself up,' the president whispered. 'I *have* to. It's the only way to keep you safe.' He turned towards the stairs.

'Mr President? Are you hiding from me?'

'No.' I grabbed his arm. 'It *isn't* the only way. I've already told you, I'm not giving you up. It's time to fight.'

'Fight?' He looked back at me. 'With what? Your bow and arrow?'

'Dad always told me I'm smart.' It felt good to know that I wasn't going to run. It made me feel strong and confident. 'You're smart too, President. Together we can beat them, I know we can. Once and for all.'

'How? You have an idea?'

'Yes, I do,' I said. 'Follow me.'

GAME PLAN

Hazar didn't call out again.

The plane settled into an eerie silence. Smoke and dust hung in the air, sparkling in the faint light that filtered around the edges of the closed blinds. Water dripped. The occasional groan of metal snaked through the cabin. From time to time something was displaced, skidding across the floor as water seeped into the plane and tipped it a little further back into oblivion.

I crouched in the darkness, bow ready, squeezed against the far end of the Presidential Suite. It was a gamble, but my instincts told me it was a good place to make our final stand. This was how it had to be.

The space was a little smaller than our living room at

home, and was triangular, coming to a flat point behind the nose of the plane. Two beds were angled in so the heads were close together, which was where I now waited, huddled low.

Dad had taught me to use my surroundings as camouflage, so that was what I had done. Sheets, pillows, cushions, and anything else I could find were strewn across the floor to create confusing shadows and shapes. A pile at the narrow end imitated not trees and bracken, but the jumbled heaps of debris that were scattered in every room of the plane. The perfect place to blend in. Nothing here would look unusual.

All I had to do now was wait.

Tap. Tap. Tap.

I raised a hand and cupped it behind my ear, turning my head slightly.

Tap. Tap.

Someone coming down the steps from the communications centre. Just one person. Heavy, but walking lightly, trying to be silent.

The sound stopped and I closed my eyes, listening.

I focused on my breathing, forcing myself to become calm.

A steady heart means a steady hand.

Whoever had come down the stairs was waiting by the door to the medical office. I pictured Morris peering into that room, knowing the layout, knowing where to look. He would scan the most obvious hiding places first – behind desks and chairs, inside cabinets. He would do the same in this room, overlooking what was hiding in plain sight.

A burst of static crackled into the silence. Short and loud.

Pssssssshhhhhht!

'You found him yet?'

Pssssssshhhhhht!

'What the hell you doing down there . . .?'

'Shhh!' came the reply, and the radio went quiet.

The plane groaned and pitched to one side, sending a shudder through the cabin. Wreckage slid across surfaces and clattered into the walls.

'Damn it,' someone said, then everything fell silent once more.

Just dripping.

And the scuff of a shoe on the carpet.

Morris was coming.

He was not a hunter; that was for sure. I could have moved along the corridor and passed the president's office without making a single sound. Not Morris, though. He probably thought he was doing well, but his shoes shuffled on the plush carpet, his clothes swished against the wall, and his breath sighed into the air. He might as well have whistled as he approached.

I knew when he was behind the door, and I raised my bow enough to pull the string back as far as I could manage in this position. I took shallow breaths and waited. Waited. Waited.

I had hunter's blood in my veins.

The darkness sparkled in my eyes, and the smoke and dust glittered.

The door scraped the carpet as it opened, making a sound like gentle waves on the lake shore. For a few seconds it was as if it had opened on its own. No one appeared. Then he was there, silhouetted in the doorway as he edged sideways, presenting as small a target as possible.

I knew, straight away, that it was not Morris. Morris was thicker-set and his hair was cropped short. He wore a suit, too. This man was wearing a tighter jacket and he was slimmer and shorter.

Hazar stood with his back to the wall as he slipped into the room, pistol raised in front of him.

'Now!' I hissed and stood up, drawing the bowstring.

As I rose, the president flicked a switch, turning on all the lights in the room, making Hazar squeeze his eyes shut in automatic response. He had seen me, though, caught a glimpse of me before he was blinded, and he swung his weapon around, squeezing the trigger.

He fired twice, making a terrible boom inside the small room. The barrel flashed, the pistol kicked, and the bullets thumped into the wall on one side of me.

I hadn't expected our attacker to react so quickly, and my survival instinct took over, making me twist away, releasing the arrow to fall harmlessly to the floor. As I moved, the plane lurched once more, making me lose my footing and bang the back of my head against the wooden table behind me. I slumped to the floor in a daze.

At the same time, the president jumped down from the desk behind the door and swung a heavy fire extinguisher at Hazar's face. The movement of the plane disrupted him, though, and gave Hazar just enough time to recover from his surprise. He reacted by leaning back and raising his arm so the fire extinguisher skimmed against his forearm and swung into the wall beside him. As soon as the president was overbalanced by the weight of the extinguisher, Hazar stepped in and brought the barrel of his pistol crashing into the president's head, breaking the skin and drawing blood.

My friend cried out in pain and put his hands to his head as he collapsed to the floor, then Hazar was on him, pinning him down and pressing the pistol under the president's left ear.

From where I was lying, stunned and bleary-eyed, I saw Hazar grit his teeth and put his left hand around the president's throat. 'At last,' he growled like an animal that had finally caught its prey.

'Please,' the president said.

Hazar glanced over in my direction and I closed my eyes, playing dead.

'Don't . . .' The president struggled to even whisper.

I risked opening my eyes a touch, repositioning my head to see what was going on. Hazar was still pinning the president to the floor, with one hand on his throat and the other holding the pistol. He was looking down at him, baring his teeth, his eyes wide in anger.

I took the chance to reach out for my bow, closing my fingers around it and pulling it closer.

Hazar pressed the pistol harder and took a deep breath. 'My orders were to take you alive, but now—'

'Orders?' Hazar's grip was so tight that the president's words were hoarse. 'What . . . orders? What the hell do you want from me?'

'I don't have time for this.' Hazar's voice was deep and savage.

'Tell me,' he insisted.

Hazar sneered and pressed the pistol harder, digging it right into the president's skin. 'It won't make any difference to you now, but this isn't how it was supposed to be.'

'Tell me,' the president asked again, trying to move his head away from the pistol.

Hazar took a deep breath and tightened his jaw so the muscles bulged in his cheeks. He glanced across at me, making me close my eyes, then growled and cleared his throat. 'You were going to be held captive. Filmed and uploaded on a live web stream, every moment of your imprisonment to be documented.'

'What?'

I opened my eyes just enough to see Hazar lean forward, so his face was a hair's breadth from the president's. The wicked smile appearing on his lips told me he was starting to feel like he had won. He had caught his prey.

'After seven days, you would be beheaded,' he said. 'The images would horrify the world and everyone would know the War on Terror is not over. The US government would double funding to the Central Intelligence Agency, extraditions could restart, and everyone would turn a blind eye to torture and interrogation. *That* was the game plan.'

'What . . . the hell . . . kind of terrorist are you? I thought you were . . . some kind of hunter.'

'That's what that idiot Morris thinks.' Hazar turned his head in my direction, making me close my eyes once more, but he was distracted now. He was enjoying himself. 'But I'm much more than that, Mr President: I'm a fixer. I fix things. I was going to make you a martyr. Everyone would love you. The United States would have its anti-terrorist budget, and there's a vice president just waiting in the wings to be sworn in.'

'*He* knows about this? *That's* how you got access to the satellite feeds? He's in on this?'

'Who do you think planned it all? And what vice president doesn't want to be president? The only way for that to happen, though, is for the president to die.'

'You don't have to do this,' the president said.

'You'd be surprised how many times I've heard that. So many people say—'

From somewhere deep in the plane came a long, cavernous groan, like the mourning of some giant beast, and everything heaved. The cabin pitched further, the tail sinking deeper, making the plane's nose rise and twist.

I opened my eyes in time to see Hazar thrown sideways off the president, his pistol raised so that the muzzle was pointed at the far wall.

Seeing his chance, the president seemed to awaken like a wild animal. It was as if the past hours of fearing for his life had finally unlocked something inside him, and now it was ready to be unleashed. He let out the most terrifying shout and exploded in a burst of unexpected strength and aggression. He turned and threw himself on Hazar, grabbing his pistol arm in one hand and using the other to rain punches down on the man's head.

'I am not going to die!' he shouted as he threw his fists at Hazar. 'I am not going to die!'

I jumped to my feet and hurried across the debris-littered floor, but the president was doing fine without me. Hazar had lost his grip on the weapon, which went skittering away to be lost among the other clutter, and was trying to protect himself. The president was like a madman, pummelling him with both fists, over and over again until Hazar stopped moving altogether. Only then did the president finally stand and step back to look down at Hazar.

'First it's my bodyguard and now it's my vice president. Who's next?'

His shoulders were moving up and down as he breathed away his fury, and his face was contorted into a grim expression of anger.

'You got him,' I said.

The president looked at me and shook himself, as if to banish the demon that had possessed him. He closed his eyes and let out a long sigh, and when he opened his eyes again he looked normal. Scared and confused, just like the man who had stepped out of the pod last night. 'Do . . . do you think he's dead?'

I crouched beside Hazar and put my index finger below his nose, feeling the heat of his breath. 'No.' I shook my head. 'But he's out cold.'

'Morris would have been proud of me,' he said, rubbing his throat.

'*I'm* proud of you.'

The radio on Hazar's belt let out a blast of static, making us both snap our heads around to look at it.

Pssssssshhhhhht!

'Hazar?' Morris's whispering voice hissed into the suite. 'Hazar? What's going on? Hazar? *Hazar?* Damn it!' The radio clicked off.

'He heard the shots,' I said. 'He knows something's wrong.'

The president's eyes widened and he stumbled over to the far wall as the plane groaned and moved again. He steadied himself with one arm, then started lifting blankets and pillows, throwing them aside.

'What are you doing?'

'The gun,' he said. 'We need to find it.'

'Forget the gun,' I said, 'you need to do something with *him*. Tie him up, or . . . something. He's going to wake up any moment.'

'What about Morris?'

'Leave him to me.' I pulled an arrow from the quiver on my back. 'I'm going to hunt him.'

'What? No, Oskari, he's too dangerous.'

I thought I could see doubt in his eyes, even after everything we'd been through, and a spark of anger and disappointment flared in me. It brought with it all the other feelings I'd had when I was standing up there on the platform, seeing everybody's faces as I tried to draw the bow.

'Why does nobody ever think I can do it?'

'It's not *that*. I just don't want anything to happen to you, Oskari.' He reached out to stop me, but I was already heading for the door.

ENDGAME

I imagined I was hunting in the forest behind our house at night. Instead of trees and shrubs to block my path, though, there were overturned chairs and piles of papers. Instead of creeping around boulders and moving silently down muddy inclines, I had to navigate bags and broken laptops, and a wet carpeted floor that sloped away towards the tail of the plane.

The bow was in my hand, an arrow nocked against the string.

I was a hunter again. No longer running, no longer afraid.

Morris was my prey.

I concentrated on my breathing, bringing it slow and steady, moving just millimetres at a time, making no noise at all. I was like the mist as I passed the president's office and ventured deeper into the darkness.

The blinds remained down, covering the windows, stopping anything but the narrowest beams of light from entering the cabin. Smoke and dust danced in the air.

He was out there. I could hear his breathing, hear the whisper of his shoes on the carpet.

There.

Close.

About a metre away.

The security door that the president had sealed when we came into the plane was now open. We had left it that way when we prepared our trap, encouraging the men to split up, and they had fallen for it. Morris was beyond the door, in the meeting area we had come through.

Shuck!

It took me a moment to realize what the sound was. The shutters. Morris was raising the shutters.

Shuck!

He was trying to take away my advantage of darkness.

Shuck!

Light flooded into the cabin.

'No more hiding in the dark, Mr President. Time to show yourself.' His quiet voice slipped along the corridor like the murmur of an evil spirit.

I stopped and moved sideways into the medical office, standing still and listening.

Shuck!

'You know I'm going to find you.'

I lifted the bow and drew the string, focusing on what I had to do. It was him or me. I had to do this. My arrow had to fly true.

Shuck!

'Nowhere to hide, Mr President.'

The string came back and back, as if my strength knew I needed it now more than ever. It came past my shoulder and across my chest. My left hand gripped the bow like a vice, my arm was like solid wood. The string cut into the fingers of my right hand as I drew it further and further. It reached the tip of my nose without faltering. Then it was as far back as any man could draw it. The string was against my cheek and the bow was at its most powerful. There was no surge of excitement, though, and my breathing didn't quicken. I had done it: I had drawn the bow. But this was not a time for celebration; it was a time for hunting.

And hunting is a serious matter.

The sound of shoe leather on the carpet. Out in the corridor this time.

Shuck!

I sidestepped out from the medical office and faced him. One step was all it took, and the bow remained solid in my hand, the string remained at my cheek, the arrow remained in my fingers.

Morris saw me right away. He took a pace towards me, then hesitated and stared in confusion.

So I shot him.

I released the arrow, strong and true, and it flew at

him along the corridor as if in slow motion. I saw every vibration of the wooden shaft and every ruffle of the feathered flight. It was a deadly missile, racing to its mark.

It struck him in the chest. A perfect shot.

But it did nothing. It hit Morris right over the heart and bounced away like a stick thrown by a child.

Morris stepped back in alarm, then stopped and glanced down. When he looked up at me, his eyes flashed and his lip curled.

'Well, well,' he said, lowering his pistol slightly. 'The small shoes.'

I stared in disbelief. I had hunted and hidden and drawn the bow as far as it would go, and yet Morris was still standing. I had failed.

'You've caused me quite a bit of trouble, kid, but now it's time to let the grown-ups get on with their business.'

'That might have been true yesterday,' I heard myself say.

'What's that?'

I swallowed hard and felt my anger returning. 'I said, "That might have been true yesterday." But today is my birthday.'

I reached over my shoulder and drew the last arrow from the quiver.

Morris watched me, the grin still in place. 'So? Why should I care?'

I nocked the arrow and lifted the bow. 'Because today is the day I become a man.'

'Seriously?' He shook his head. 'A bow and arrow

against Kevlar? Jesus, you probably don't even know what that is, do you?' He tapped his chest with his left hand. 'Bullet. Proof. Vest. Idiot.'

I began to draw the string back.

'I'm glad you became a man today,' Morris said, starting to raise his weapon. 'Because it means I won't be killing a . . .'

The grin was gone in an instant. His eyes widened and his cheeks changed colour.

'. . . a . . .' His body hitched as if he'd been punched.

'. . . a . . .' He put his hand up to his chest and made a strange gagging noise as he fell to his knees.

'. . . a . . . kid.'

Morris knelt in front of me, swaying from side to side, then his whole body tensed as if he'd been electrocuted. He keeled over to the left, releasing his weapon and sliding back against the wall.

I was still standing there, bow drawn, when the president came half running, half sliding down the sloping corridor behind me. He bumped into me, making me drop the arrow, which slipped away and disappeared among the debris that had piled against the far wall.

'Oskari, are you all right?' He stopped beside me and put his hand on my arm, encouraging me to lower the bow. 'My God, Oskari, you've got some guts. You just faced down Morris, a member of the president's security detail. Those guys are seriously badass, and he was the best of them.'

'I . . . what . . .? Did I kill him?' I didn't understand what had happened.

'He was already dead,' the president told me. 'Bullet fragment near his heart, remember? All this excitement must have moved it and—'

'Did I kill him?' I asked again, turning to stare at him.

His face softened. 'No, Oskari. He was already dead. Trust me.'

The plane gave a long groan beneath us, louder than we'd heard before, and lurched for the last time before it began sliding back into the lake.

The sound of gushing water filled the cabin and we looked along the length of the corridor to see the lake rushing up through the plane to meet us. Air Force One was about to slip away from the shallows and disappear into the depths of the lake.

'We're sinking!' the president yelled. 'We've got to get out of here!'

GAME OVER

'**W**hat about Hazar?' I shouted as we hurried back towards the president's office. 'Did you tie him?'

'Yes.'

'He'll drown.'

'Nothing we can do about that now,' he replied. 'No time. Got to save ourselves.' He stopped by the exit and grabbed the red lever. 'You're more important, Oskari. Hazar will have to take his chances.' He twisted the lever and swung the door out, letting in a blast of cold air that reeked of aviation fuel.

There was something else, too – the sound of the helicopter hovering overhead. I had forgotten all about it because we hadn't been able to hear it inside the sealed aircraft, but now it made me hesitate. Hazar's men were still up there, waiting for their boss.

'Jump!' the president shouted.

I looked down at the surface of the lake.

'Now!' He shoved me out.

Bow in hand, I hit the water and went under as the president splashed down beside me. We surfaced together to take a gulp of stinking air and swam away from the plane, heading towards the shore.

The helicopter continued to hover overhead, waiting hopelessly for Hazar to complete his mission.

'We have to go under,' I said. 'They'll see us.'

The president nodded, and we took a deep breath before diving down and swimming as far as we could before resurfacing for air. When we were a few metres away, I came up for breath and looked back to see the plane slowly disappearing beneath the lake. The tail that had once been standing proud, emblazoned with the US flag, was now gone, and the scorched area at the rear of the plane had sunk out of sight, too. It was like the lake was eating Air Force One.

I ducked back under and watched through the murky gloom as the massive bulk of the aircraft slipped backwards like a dying beast. The water seemed to boil as bubbles rushed around it, escaping from the air pockets that had saved our lives. The lights continued to flicker and blink, flashing red and green and yellow. Many were almost out of sight now, though, unable to pierce the darkness into which they were falling. A few more minutes and the plane would be at the bottom of the lake, taking Morris and Hazar with it.

When I resurfaced again, the president was looking back at his plane, too. Everything behind the wings was gone now; all that remained in view was the front part of the aircraft, where his office and suite were located, and the communications centre and flight deck above.

The helicopter continued to hover overhead, casting ripples across the lake.

'Come on,' I said, shivering. 'We can't let them see us.'

The president watched for a moment longer, then dived under and followed me as we swam for the shore, passing beneath the countless dead fish flashing silver on the waves above.

The water was greasy with fuel, and each time we came up for breath the stink of it hurt my nostrils and made me light-headed. As we came closer to the shore, though, it lessened, gradually washing off our skin and clothing each time we went under.

I couldn't believe we had beaten Hazar and Morris – but I also couldn't help thinking about Hazar tied up in the president's suite, panicking as the plane dragged him down to his death. There was something else, too: the constant presence of the men in the helicopter. All it would take was for one of them to look across the water and see us making our escape.

When we were close to the bank, I glanced back to see the helicopter hovering over what was left of the plane. It was almost gone now – the door we had jumped from was beneath the water, and the nose of the jet was at a more severe angle, pointing to the tops of the stunted trees on the small lake island that had kept Air Force One afloat during the night.

But something caught my attention.

Some kind of movement.

I blinked water from my eyes and looked again. Maybe it had been a curious bird, or debris swept up by the helicopter's downdraught.

There it was again, though. Movement in the plane's cockpit window.

'What's that?' I said, wiping my face, trying to clear my vision.

The president stopped beside me and turned to watch. 'I don't see any—'

Something seemed to grow from the window. A dark shape that pushed upwards like a moth emerging from a chrysalis.

'Hazar,' I said. It had to be.

'I tied him up.'

'Not well enough.'

As we watched, Hazar pulled himself through the broken cockpit window and crawled on to the nose of the jet. He paused, then got to his feet and looked out across the lake in our direction.

'He can't see us,' the president said.

But Hazar lifted a hand and pointed right at us, then turned and signalled to the men in the helicopter.

'Yes, he can,' I said.

One of the soldiers leaned out and handed something down to Hazar. Part of a weapon I had seen before.

'Start swimming,' I said. 'Now.'

We both turned and began swimming as fast as we could towards the shore. I knew what Hazar would do next. He would put that rifle together, fitting each part into place, and it wouldn't take him long.

'Faster!' I shouted at the president, who was starting to fall behind. We were both exhausted, but I had something to make me swim faster – I knew what a good shot Hazar was. I had seen Patu run for his life and fail.

We made it to the shallows and put our feet down on the soft ground, wading quickly on to the shore. The muddy bank was open and clear for twenty metres or so before the treeline of the forest. Here and there, piles of driftwood lay like old bones, and craggy rocks and boulders littered the dirt as if they had been dropped from the sky. Those giant stones were the only cover available between the shore and the forest.

'Keep going!' I shouted. 'To the rocks!'

We ran and stumbled to a collection of dark grey boulders, reaching them and diving for cover as Hazar's first shot hit the ground halfway up the shore. It whizzed past us and smacked into the mud with a soft thump that sprayed a great gout of mud into the grey air. The sound of the gunshot reached us a fraction of a second later, a loud *CRACK!* that echoed around the lake, sending birds into the sky above the trees.

If we had been any slower, the shot would have hit the president.

'He got out?' he said. 'How the hell did he get out?'

'Doesn't matter,' I said. 'It's not important.'

I crawled along the ground and risked a peek through the narrow gap between two rocks. The helicopter was still there, hovering, and Hazar was standing by the plane's cockpit window, rifle to his shoulder.

That was all I saw before I pulled away. And it was just as well, because Hazar had spotted me. As I moved back, a bullet struck the gap between the rocks, spraying sharp fragments and passing through to hit the mud behind me with a thump.

Once again, the sound of the shot cracked in the air a moment later.

'He has a good scope,' I said. 'And he's a good shot.'

'Oh my God,' the president said. 'Is this ever going to end?'

'Yes,' I said. 'It is.'

If we tried to make it to the treeline, Hazar would kill us. If we tried to make it to the water, Hazar would kill us. If we stayed where we were, Hazar would get into his helicopter and come over to kill us.

The only thing left was for us to attack.

I remembered what Dad had taught me, what he had reminded me about yesterday when we had driven up to the Place of Skulls. The two most important things. My knife and my fire kit.

As long as you have those two things, you can survive anywhere and anything. Carry them on you at all times. Never put them in your pack, and don't lose them. Out there, they can be the difference between life and death.

My knife and my fire kit.

And my bow.

'I have an idea,' I said. 'Get me a stick.'

'What?'

'A *stick*. Arrow-length.'

While the president shuffled over to the pile of drift-wood behind us, I slipped my knife from its sheath and put it on the ground in front of me. I then took the fire kit from my zipped pocket, relieved to see that the water-proof tub was still sealed tight.

'Will this do?' the president said, holding up a slightly crooked stick.

'It'll have to.' I used my knife to shorten it and notch a groove into one end. I quickly sharpened the other end to a point with two or three rapid cuts. With that done, I cut a thin strip from the hem of my shirt and put it between my teeth while I twisted open the waterproof tub.

'Knife and a fire kit,' the president said, starting to understand.

I nodded without looking at him, and took out the storm-proof matches.

'I guess this counts as an emergency, right?' he asked.

'Right,' I said through clamped teeth.

I cracked the seal on the yellow container and took out four of the matches.

I put them around the sharpened end of the arrow and held them in place with my left hand, using my right to take the strip of shirt from my mouth. Wrapping the cotton around the matches, I tied them to the stick with a simple knot, then nocked the makeshift arrow to my bow.

There were no feathered flights, and the stick was too crooked to fly straight, but I hoped it would be enough. It was all we had left.

Shifting on to my knees, I drew the bow back, gritting my teeth and calling on all the strength I had left. My arms shook, but I put every bit of energy into it. I had to make this count. It was our last chance.

When the string touched my cheek for the second time that day, I knew my plan would work.

'Light it,' I said, leaning back, angling the arrow towards the sky.

The president already had a match in his hand, and he struck it on the side of the container. When he touched it to the tip of the arrow, the other four matches flared with a whisper. I watched until I was certain they were alight, then I released the string.

Without flights, the arrow spun and twisted as it flew, but it sailed high. Propelled by the full power of the bow, it went up and up, arcing over the rocks, over the mud and over the lake until it finally began to descend, falling out of view.

Then, above the sound of the helicopter, we heard the distinctive *WHUMP!* of fuel catching fire, and large flames leaped into view over the top of the boulders.

'It worked,' I whispered, and scrambled over to the gap in the rocks.

What I saw through that gap was like Hell.

'Look!' I grabbed the president's arm, and together we stood to see the surface of the lake burning and dancing in a huge wall of flame. Everything in front of us was on fire, flickering in places, erupting into huge columns in others. The inferno was alive, racing from place to place on the lake, hungrily burning every drop of leaked aviation fuel as it streaked towards the plane.

We couldn't see Hazar. The flames were too high. We could see the helicopter, though. We saw the way the rotor blades fanned the blaze as the aircraft tried to rise into the sky, but it was too late. The fire burned too fast and hot for anything to survive. It smothered the plane, engulfing its fuel-covered body, sucking into every air space, racing into the fuel tanks, and detonating in a massive eruption.

The helicopter was engulfed by the ball of flame, wrapped in the orange-and-black cloud that blew high into the sky. It spun and buffeted, then it added to the explosion, blowing outwards into a thousand pieces.

The heat and the blast flashed back across the surface of the lake, peppering the shore with debris. Pieces of metal and plastic shot in all directions like a thousand bullets. The rocks sheltered us from the worst of it, but they couldn't protect us from the concussive wave that knocked us off our feet. Nor could they protect us from the rain of fragments that came pouring down from the hellish, burning sky, thumping into the mud and scattering into the trees beyond.

Everything was overcome with heat and noise and smoke, and in the midst of the hurricane of fire, there was a sharp bump on my head and a moment of pain.

TRADITION IS TRADITION

There was no thought or feeling at all, just a slow falling through never-ending space. But soon the emptiness was filled with the smell of burning fuel. A grim, ugly smell that slipped its fingers down my throat and blackened my lungs. It scratched its nails along my throat, making me cough. With that came the dull throbbing at the back of my head, and I remembered that I had hit it when . . . when had it been? Yesterday? A year ago?

No, not that long. In the president's suite. I had jumped up to distract a man called Hazar and . . .

'President?' I opened my eyes and sat up. 'President?'

He was lying beside me, pressed against the rocks and curled into a ball. His face was covered and his hands were wrapped over his head.

'President?'

Smoke drifted around us, thick and black, and the ground was littered with pieces of twisted metal and broken plastic. The sound of crackling flames made me look back to see a series of small fires burning at the treeline, reminding me of last night's plane crash. Tangled piles of driftwood were on fire, too, as if the whole world was going up in a blaze.

'President? You alive?'

I couldn't think straight. Dazed by the thunderous explosion, I felt as if my brain had been scrambled in my head and everything was fuzzy. There was something, though: a familiar sound that was growing louder by the second.

Thucka-thucka-thucka.

A helicopter.

NO! The word screamed through my head. They couldn't have survived. I saw them explode . . . I saw them burn up and burst into a thousand pieces. Not even Hazar could have survived that.

The sound came closer, thumping across the lake towards us, and I leaned back to see two helicopters flying side by side.

More hunters. More men coming to take my friend.

I pushed to my feet, wobbling with dizziness and putting a hand on the rocks to support myself as I watched them reach the shore and hover like giant black insects.

Smoke swirled in tornadoes beneath them as ropes dropped down from either side and men in black zipped down, armed with assault rifles and sub-machine guns.

'No,' I said, moving away from the rocks and stumbling into the open to meet them. They weren't going to have him. He was mine. 'No.' I reached down to grasp the handle of my knife and pull it free of its sheath. 'No.'

'It's all right,' said a voice behind me, and I turned to see the president standing there. His face was bloody and his clothes were tattered. He reached out and put a hand on mine, stopping me from drawing the blade. 'These guys are with me.'

I tried to pull the knife anyway, but he held my hand firm and shook his head. 'They found us, Oskari. The rescue party. It's time to go home.'

Beyond the rocks, close to the waterline, three of the soldiers remained on the ground beneath the helicopter, facing in different directions, watching for threats. Another four hustled towards us with their weapons pointed at me. As they came closer, the president limped forward and held up a hand.

'Am I glad to see you. Stand down, Captain,' he said, but his voice was quiet and they ignored the order. They moved between us, escorting the president away while others continued to point their guns at me, and I wondered if they had really come to rescue us. Maybe they were more of Hazar's men.

'I said, "Stand down, Captain"!' the president ordered, raising his voice and pulling himself away from them. 'And take good care of this young man.' He came back to me and pushed the soldiers aside to put a hand on my shoulder. 'If it wasn't for him, you'd have a new president now.'

The captain glanced down at me with a serious look. He had square features and cropped hair. His brow was furrowed into a frown, and he gave me a curt nod before looking back at the president. 'Sir, please come with us. We have a jet at Rovaniemi airport waiting to take you to Helsinki.'

The president nodded and looked at me, reassuring me that it was all right, and the soldiers surrounded us while we waited for one of the helicopters to touch down. Once it was on the ground, the men escorted us back along the shore towards it.

'Wait!' I said, suddenly remembering something. 'My bow!'

One of the soldiers turned to grab me, but the president stopped him, saying, 'Let him go.'

I ran back to the rocks and searched through the sticks and other wreckage until I found the bow that Hamara had handed to me on the platform yesterday. I could hardly believe it had only been a day since I had left Dad behind and ventured into the forest alone.

'Can't forget that,' the president said, glancing down at the bow as we climbed aboard the helicopter.

We sat opposite one another and the soldiers buckled us into our seats. I put the bow across my knees and looked at the battered and bruised president. Within seconds the helicopter lifted off the ground, rising high above the lake, then turned, put its nose down, and sped off across the trees.

'I want you to contact the Pentagon and have the vice president arrested,' the president said to the captain. 'Do it now.' He didn't sound so much like my president now; he sounded like a man who was used to giving orders rather than a man who needed to be led through the wilderness.

'Sir.' The captain spoke into his communicator, passing on the message.

'And we won't be going to Rovaniemi.' The president kept his eyes on me as he shouted over the noise of the helicopter.

'Sir, those are our orders,' said the captain. 'From there you'll be taken to—'

'That's not where we're going.' Still he didn't look at the soldiers. 'We're going to take Oskari home first.'

'If you mean this boy, sir, then we can take him home after—'

'I know you're just doing your job, Captain.' The president shifted his eyes to look at the soldier sitting beside him. It was a look that dared the man to disobey him. 'But remember who I am. You take your orders from me, and I am ordering you to take this young man home. It's the least I can do for him.'

The captain paused.

'Do you understand?'

'Sir, yes, sir. Um . . . you have a location on that? We need to know where "home" is, sir.'

The president looked at me and raised his eyebrows.

'Where do you want to go, Oskari?'

'The Place of Skulls.'

'The *what*?' The president looked surprised and leaned closer as if he hadn't heard me properly.

'The Place of Skulls,' I repeated. 'That's where Dad will be waiting for me.'

'I thought that's what you said. Sounds like a serious place.'

'It is.'

The president nodded and turned to the captain. 'You heard the man. Take us to the Place of Skulls.'

'Um. You have coordinates on that?' asked the captain.

'South-west of the lake,' I said.

The captain spoke the directions into his microphone, relaying them to the pilot. Immediately, the helicopter banked east.

'No coordinates?' the captain asked. 'Nothing else?'

I shook my head, wondering how I could explain where to go. 'Wait,' I said, unbuckling my seat belt and turning to look out of the window behind me.

The wilderness was whipping away beneath us at an incredible rate as we skimmed across the tops of the trees. Staring at the vast sea of trees and mountains around us, I searched for something familiar.

'Come into the cockpit,' the president said, unbuckling himself and taking me forwards.

'Sir,' the captain warned, 'I really must ask you to—' One look from the president was all it took. He stopped what he was saying, nodded and saluted. 'Sir.'

254

We moved forward to the cockpit, looking over the pilot's shoulder, seeing Lake Tuonela below. From this height it looked even bigger than I had imagined. Like the sea. The mist had cleared and the weak sunlight sparkled on the surface. Close to the shore, the water was still burning, and there was a dark shape drifting below the surface.

I looked up at the president and knew he was thinking about all the people who had been on the aircraft. Hazar and Morris might have deserved to go down with it, but the others hadn't.

'Sir,' the captain said to him. 'I've just had word from the Pentagon. The vice president was found dead in the bathroom a few moments ago. Apparently he slipped on some soap and struck his head.'

'Soap?'

'That's the information I have, sir.'

'Have you ever slipped on soap in the bathroom, Captain?'

'Can't say I have, sir.'

'Me neither. I think maybe someone *helped* him slip. The kind of person who helped him organize this set-up, because God knows he couldn't be this devious on his own. Someone silenced the vice president, *inside the Pentagon*, and whoever it was, they're probably still in there now.' The president thought for a moment. 'Captain, have security lock the place down. Someone there knows who set me up.'

'Lock it down sir? The whole Pentagon?'

'Those are my orders. Get it done.'

'Sir, yes, sir.'

We flew past the waterfall and I pointed, showing the pilot which way to go: over the top of the mountain, down past the scars in the forest where the planes had crashed, and then on to where Dad would be waiting.

When we came to the Place of Skulls, I couldn't believe how small it looked.

Yesterday it had seemed so big, it was my whole world. Now it just looked like a ramshackle platform and a collection of battered caravans, dented SUVs, and temporary shelters.

It was my place, though. Dad was there, and that gave me the best feeling. I was home.

The noise had drawn the men out of their shelters and caravans, and they were all standing, necks craned and hands over their brows, to watch our approach. Hamara was there, unmistakable, and Davi who had almost knocked me off my feet yesterday when he slapped me on the back. I could see some of the older boys there, too, Risto and Broki shielding their eyes as they looked up, and my friends Jalmar and Onni standing near them.

The pilot circled the helicopter once over the Place of Skulls, and as we finally came to a hover and began to descend I saw Dad standing beside our SUV, rifle over his shoulder. When we touched the ground, the president ordered the pilot to switch off the engine, then we went back into the body of the helicopter as the captain drew back the door and jumped down, weapon trained on the hunters. The other soldiers disembarked next, some crouching, some standing and moving away in an arc, keeping their weapons ready.

When I jumped down, I saw the shock and surprise on Dad's face. I had never seen him look that way before and it brought tears to my eyes. I was so relieved to be home, to see him again, and knew that he felt the same.

He stood by the SUV for a second in disbelief, then came forward, slowly at first, but then breaking into a jog.

One of the soldiers stepped into his path, pointing his weapon at Dad's chest.

'That's my son!' Dad shouted, and raised a hand to point. 'My son!'

I wanted to run to him, too, but I stopped myself. There was something I had to do first.

It was tradition.

I wiped my tears and stood tall and strong, gripping the bow in my right hand and keeping my eyes forwards as I strode across the Place of Skulls, past the other boys and men.

I marched straight towards Hamara and stood in front of him, looking into his eyes.

'The traditional bow,' I said, holding it out to him.

Hamara opened his mouth, but no words came out. He looked at me, then at the soldiers and the helicopter. Then he looked at the man who had come to stand beside me.

'The traditional bow,' I said again, trying to make him look down at me. 'And I have brought this man out of the forest. This is my trophy. This is what the forest has given me.'

'Are you . . .?' He couldn't take his eyes off the president. 'Are you . . .?'

'The traditional bow,' I said once more, grasping Hamara's hand and pressing the weapon into his fingers.

Finally he took the bow and looked down at me. 'Is that . . .?'

I didn't reply. I left him standing there open-mouthed, and walked over to Dad, taking the president with me.

'Oskari?' Dad looked stunned and confused and concerned all at once. I'd never seen such a look on his face. 'What's going on?'

'Dad, I want you meet someone,' I said. 'This is . . .' I hesitated. 'This is Bill.'

The president stepped forward and held out his hand.

'Bill?' Dad said, looking from me to the president and then back again.

'Bill,' the president confirmed. 'And you're Tapio?'

Lost for words, Dad could only nod as he put out a hesitant hand and shook with the president.

'I've heard about you,' the president said. 'Oskari tells me you're an amazing hunter. Well, just so you know' – he took his hand from Dad's and rested it on my shoulder – 'so is your son. He's pretty good at saving presidents, too.'

'You saved the president?' Tears welled in Dad's eyes as he looked down at me. 'You brought the *president* out of the forest?'

'There's something I need to tell you, though,' I said. 'I crashed the ATV. I think it's—'

'I don't care about that.' Dad suddenly seemed to come to life. He grabbed me and pulled me to him, hugging me tight. He leaned down to put his bristly cheek against mine and he spoke into my ear. 'Damn it, Oskari, the President of America? Mum would be so proud of you. *I'm* so proud . . . but . . . couldn't you have just settled for that buck?'

A cough and I looked around to see Hamara standing behind us with a camera in his hand. He shrugged and gave us an embarrassed smile. 'Tradition is tradition.'

PHOTOGRAPH

For a few days, everything was crazy. After the military helicopters left and the soldiers were gone, and the president was whisked away, our village was swamped by vans and cameras and people with microphones. They all wanted to ask me a million questions about what had happened. They talked to Dad and Hamara, and they filmed the village, and followed the Finnish and American authorities lifting Air Force One from the lake.

The investigation teams set up a base just outside the village, and the sky was filled with the thump and buzz of helicopters. When those sounds filtered through the air above the village at night, my dreams were filled with images of Hazar and Morris and fire in the wilderness. I always awoke from those nightmares to hear strange noises rising from Mount Akka as they dragged the aircraft from the depths of the lake and cut it into pieces to take it away.

Two days after I brought the president out of the forest as my trophy, a soldier came to our door.

Dad and I were at the window, watching the reporters and film crews waiting patiently for us to come out. I was looking at everyone and wondering if there was anything else I could say to them. I had already told them everything I was allowed to; the president's team had been clear about that.

The soldier who pushed through the throng that day was stern-faced and clean-shaven, with a crisp and perfect uniform. Under his arm, he carried a large flat parcel wrapped in brown paper. He came straight to our door and knocked three times.

Dad looked at me and left the room. He answered the door, and there was a murmur of voices before the soldier left and the door closed with a click. When Dad came back, the soldier had already disappeared into the crowd.

'It's for you.' Dad held out the parcel.

'What is it?' I hesitated before taking it from him and putting it on the table, carefully unwrapping the paper to reveal what was inside.

'I know just where to put that.' Dad smiled and pushed back his cap. 'Get your coat.'

When we left the house, I carried the parcel under my arm, just as the soldier had done, wrapped up once more in the brown paper. Dad walked by my side and we ignored the reporters, pushing through them and heading up the road towards the end of the village. The road was lined with cars belonging to the visitors, as well as the rusted pickups and rickety caravans of those of us who lived here. As we passed the other homes, all of them wooden and ordinary, like our own, some of the reporters followed, cameras held at the ready, shoving one another to get close to us.

I didn't say anything to them, though. I just kept my eyes ahead and walked on through the sunny afternoon, feeling the fresh air on my face.

When we reached the end of the village, we stopped outside the Hunting Lodge. Twice as big as our house, it was the largest building in the village, built on two storeys, from huge timbers that looked as ancient as those of the platform in the Place of Skulls. It was where the men came almost every night, and until now it had mostly been out of bounds for me. I had only ever been inside a few times.

'You go in first,' Dad said.

The door squeaked when I pushed it open and stepped in.

I glanced around, seeing the men sitting at the tables. Tough and hardened hunters, bearded and weather-beaten. Some leaned close together in quiet discussion, others were drunk and laughing together. The wooden walls surrounding them were decorated with the antlers and skulls of prized animals, each one with its own story to tell. The air was thick with the smell of tobacco smoke and stale beer and sweat.

Sitting alone at the bar, Hamara was the first to see us enter.

As usual, he was wearing his woollen hat, pulled low so that his straggly grey hair stuck out beneath it. His great beard was messy and his coat was open, revealing his dirty sweater and his bulging belly. In his right hand he held a large mug of beer. He glared at the reporters pushing in behind us, then turned his gaze on me.

When the other men spotted us, a wave of silence washed over the room until the only sound was the subdued murmur from the TV in the corner behind the bar.

Dad nudged me forward and we began walking towards the far wall. My boots were loud on the wooden floor. Everyone's eyes were on me, but it was Hamara's I felt the most. They were like hot beams boring into me.

When I came alongside him, I stopped and made myself look him in the eye.

He returned the stare, tightening his lips as he watched me, then a hint of a smile appeared and the creases at the edges of his mouth tightened. 'Oskari,' he said with a slight nod. 'I misjudged you.'

'Yes.'

'I doubted you.'

'Yes.'

'Well, I don't think anyone will make that mistake again.' He cleared his throat. 'And I've been thinking about what kind of man it makes you. A bear means strength, a buck means brains, but a president?' He raised his eyebrows and puffed out his cheeks. 'You've got me stumped.' His smile widened and he let out a small laugh as he glanced at Dad, before looking at me once more. 'You have something for the wall?'

'I do.'

'Better get to it then, young man. Tradition is tradition.'

He gestured towards the far end of the lodge, watching as Dad and I went to the back wall and looked up at the pictures of all the hunters with their trophies. There was Hamara as a thirteen-year-old boy, kneeling beside his deer. Davi with his grouse, Jalmar with his rabbits, and other boys posing with hares, pike, wood grouse, red grouse, and elk.

At the top of the wall was the photo of Dad with his bear, put back in its rightful place. It was more faded now, creased and water-damaged from my adventure, but it was where it was supposed to be.

To one side of the photos, the traditional bow hung on the wall beside the quiver I had carried across my back.

'Your picture,' Hamara said, coming to stand beside me, and he put out his hand.

I took the parcel from under my arm and removed the brown paper before handing it to Hamara. He studied it for a moment, nodding with approval, then stepped forward and reached up to hang it on a nail, higher than all the other photos.

Dad put his hand on my shoulder and I straightened my back as I looked up at the framed newspaper cutting from the *Washington Post*. The headline read:

13-YEAR-OLD FINNISH HUNTER RESCUES THE PRESIDENT OF THE UNITED STATES

Below the words was a photograph of the president lying on the ground like a hunter's prey, looking tired and scruffy, but propped up on one elbow and smiling at the camera. I was standing over him, holding the traditional hunting bow. Behind us there was a squad of Special Forces soldiers and two Black Hawk helicopters. Other helicopters hovered over the treetops in the background.

It was the photo that Hamara had taken the day I rescued Bill. The day I showed the world what kind of man I was going to be.

ACKNOWLEDGEMENTS

The time and effort poured into a novel does not come only from the author. There are lots of other people involved in the process of bringing a book to the shelf, so I'd like to take a moment to say thank you to everyone who has had a hand in making *Big Game* what it is. Thanks especially to the brilliant Barry Cunningham for introducing me to Oskari and presenting me with such a great opportunity. Thanks also to Jalmari Helander and Petri Jokiranta for giving Oskari his first breath of life, and to Will Clarke for letting me run with Oskari's story. Thanks to all the Chickens, particularly Rachel L for her insightful and invaluable advice and editorial support, and to Rachel H and Elinor for all their amazing hard work. Thanks also to my agent, Carolyn. Most of all, though, thanks to my first readers and biggest supporters – my wife and children. They are my first opinion and my last opinion, and they are the ones who have to put up with my vacant stares and memory loss when I disappear into Danworld.

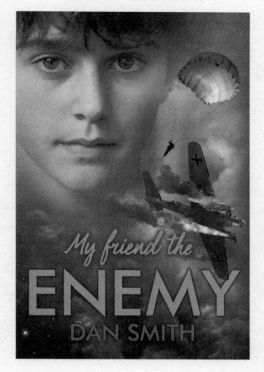

MY FRIEND THE ENEMY by DAN SMITH

1941. It's wartime and when a German plane crashes in flames near Peter's home, he rushes over hoping to find something exciting to keep.

But what he finds instead is an injured young airman. He needs help, but can either of them trust the enemy?

. . . an exciting, thought-provoking book.
THE BOOKSELLER

Paperback, ISBN 978-1-908435-81-1, £6.99 • ebook, ISBN 978-1-909489-06-6, £6.99

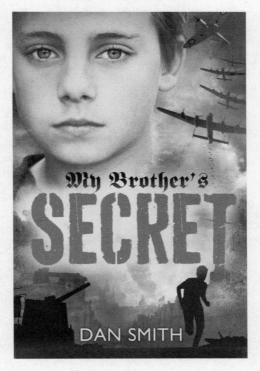

MY BROTHER'S SECRET by DAN SMITH

Twelve-year-old Karl is a good German boy. He wants his country to win the war – after all, his father has gone away to fight. But when tragedy strikes and his older brother Stefan gets into trouble, he begins to lose his faith in Hitler. Before long, he's caught up in a deadly rebellion.

Rich in detail, this is a thought-provoking story.
JULIA ECCLESHARE

Paperback, ISBN 978-1-909489-03-5, £6.99 • ebook, ISBN 978-1-909489-54-7, £6.99

THE MAZE RUNNER by JAMES DASHNER

When the doors of the lift crank open, the only thing Thomas can remember is his first name. But he's not alone. He's surrounded by boys who welcome him to the Glade, an encampment at the centre of a bizarre maze.

Like Thomas, the Gladers don't know why or how they came to be there, or what's happened to the world outside. All they know is that every morning when the walls slide back, they will risk everything to find out . . .

A dark and gripping tale of survival set in a world where teenagers fight for their lives on a daily basis.

PUBLISHERS WEEKLY

Paperback, ISBN 978-1-909489-40-0, £7.99 • ebook, ISBN 978-1-908435-48-4, £7.99

ALSO AVAILABLE:

THE SCORCH TRIALS
Paperback, ISBN 978-1-909489-41-7, £7.99 • ebook, ISBN 978-1-908435-49-1, £7.99

THE DEATH CURE
Paperback, ISBN 978-1-909489-42-4, £7.99 • ebook, ISBN 978-1-908435-35-4, £7.99

THE KILL ORDER
Paperback, ISBN 978-1-909489-43-1, £7.99 • ebook, ISBN 978-1-908435-69-9, £7.99